Heaven Scent

Love Letters From Beyond

SUZY BOOTZ

First Printing 2014

ISBN 978-0-692-23224-8

ATTENTION CORPORATIONS, UNIVERSITIES, COLLEGES, AND PROFESSIONAL ORGANIZATIONS: Quantity discounts are available on bulk purchases of this book for educational, gift purposes, or as premiums for increasing magazine subscriptions or renewals. Special book or book excerpts can also be created to fit specific needs. For information, please contact suzy@suzybootz.com.

DEDICATION

This book is dedicated to my husband and soul mate Jason, who encourages me to reach beyond my own expectations and achieve my greatest dreams.

To my mom who has taught me that nothing separates the love of a mother from her child; not in life and not even in death.

Contents

My Dearest Sophia,

After several moments of staring at a blank piece of paper, I am still at a loss of what to say to you right now. I know that as you read this letter, I am at the hospital undergoing my very first chemotherapy treatment. We thought we were 'home free' since my first cancer battle when you were only ten years old, but life has an amazing way of throwing us a curve ball when we think we are safe. My heart breaks for you as I Know how upset you are yet another diagnosis, words cannot convey the sadness I feel for you and the fear I know you must be feeling – as I am experiencing these emotions as well. Since you have always been so open to our letters, then I wanted to write you so when you are ready to read these words you will be more receptive to them. Sophia, you are so much like me, that when you are upset about something you tend to shut down and not listen to anyone.

First of all, I want to thank you for being my best friend and for handling my first battle with breast cancer like such an adult. I know it was so hard for you, but you trusted God that somehow our journey would allow us to grow closer and we were allowed to spend every day that we have had in absolute gratitude. Had we not been given a reason to appreciate life, our bond may have never grown to the magnitude that it has. Now as you sit in your room, where you spend all of your worrisome moments and read this letter once again trying to understand how we now have to endure another journey through this battle.

This letter allows you to read and understand these words when you are ready to do so. I know that my being diagnosed with breast cancer is something that is completely out of your control and it isn't fair. Life often presents itself as being unfair, but the fair part of this situation is that I am still here today to be your mom and love and hold you every night. Some people have not been afforded that opportunity today my beautiful daughter.

Since the doctor's visit this past week, I know what fear is and to be honest I am scared to pieces. I have learned to start praying again in ways that I never thought were imaginable, and Sophia this act of prayer is getting me through the most difficult part of my emotions this week. I have realized that fear is almost a waste of time because it is energy that I don't have to waste. Fear is about not being present in the moment, because whatever is happening at this particular moment in my life or yours we are able to control how we choose to react to it. When we think about the future moments, fear is allowed to take control over our mind and run free.

I cannot afford to allow my mind to run in fear because in these past few days, it has taken me to darkness unknown. Promise yourself that during this time you will take each moment as it comes and not be in fear of the unknown. Realizing that your energy is being spent on an illusion of time that doesn't exist will allow you to have some control over an experience that you believe you have no control over my child.

Life is a precious gift and I am writing this letter to you today, very much alive and now more than ever before, being in a state of gratitude. I am thankful for each moment with you Sophia and every moment with your dad that I used to take for granted. I am also very grateful for my life and the moments I have to express myself in freedom of love, words, emotions, and *actions. None of us know how this disease will progress but what I do know is that this moment is all we have.*

Be present in this moment and appreciate the small things in life you once took for granted. Be thankful for your healthy body, your intelligent mind, and your loving heart. Be thankful for the doctors who are fighting along with me to beat this disease and for the many people and organizations that are offering their support to us during a difficult time like this.

Sophia, whatever you do please promise yourself that you will never lose your faith. You have the ability to turn your most painful experiences into your greatest achievement, and how you handle this difficult situation will determine how your moments with me are spent. I have realized that we each hold the pen and can write how the chapters in our lives are created. We cannot control those things that appear to be part of Gods plan but we can control how we react to them.

Take the pages of your life and write out how you want to experience these moments sentence by sentence and page by page. On some days you may find it difficult to even speak your voice and on others you may want to shout your anger out on the rooftop, but you hold the pen in your hand still. How are you going to write this chapter in your precious book of life? Are you going to close your eyes and pretend that you have no control or are you going to celebrate each and every word you write because now you understand that life on this journey is a gift that is not to be taken for granted?

For the next several months the pages may be easier for you to write on some days and others you may have difficulty remembering that you even hold the pen in your hands. Allow yourself to be human and give yourself permission to be sad, but realize that you do hold the pen and how you react to this experience through your thoughts, emotions, and actions is completely in your control.

The present moment is literally a gift, so be appreciative of each and every moment we get to share together at this time. See your life experience now through a new perspective and realize that I love you with all of my heart. I hope that somehow through this journey, you and I will grow closer to each other and you and God will grow closer as well. Realize that you gain solace by allowing yourself to connect to our creator and gaining strength from within that divine presence. I am so proud of you my beautiful daughter and whether I am in the same room as you or in a hospital bed attached to a bag of fluids, know that I am only a thought away.

I love you forever,

Momma

Sophia Rose
Chapter 1

Sophia was not your typical teenage girl, although in this uncomfortable age, she was discovering herself through her hobbies and slowly but painfully growing into her own body. At age fourteen, Sophia was taller than most girls her age and nearly taller than every boy in the entire school, which caused Sophia to become more self-conscious of her body than she already was. Because of her tall and lean frame, Sophia was easily noticed in the school hallways; however, her outgoing, bubbly personality made her a friend to most.

Sophia's height wasn't the only physical trait she had that made her stand out, she had what others referred to as large brown "doe-like eyes," that lit up whenever she spoke about fashion or her mom. Sophia's had a smile that could light up a room and she was always smiling because she was a very happy girl. She learned from her parents to always be in an attitude of gratitude because despite any situation, there was always someone somewhere who had it much worse than she did.

Sophia looked very much like a model in the making and her sense of style is what kept her interested in the latest fashion trends. She studied magazines, designer websites, and the latest celebrity trends so she could always reinvent herself. Sophia wouldn't dream of leaving the house without being completely put together. In the small town she lived in, she was known as a fashion trend setter. Rather than becoming offended that so many girls wanted to copy her clothes and latest trends, Sophia was willing to share the boutiques she found her latest style secrets and even helped some girls revamp their closets from some trendy second hand stores and accessory boutiques.

Sophia knew she wanted to be a designer or a high fashion stylist one day and her love for helping others dress in ways that made them look and feel good was what she lived for. Although high fashion was always near her heart, Sophia excelled at school. School was enjoyable for Sophia and making good grades seemed easy because she was so detail oriented and loved to study, she found that she could combine both skills to increase her GPA.

To say that Sophia was popular was an understatement as she seemed like a social chameleon. Her innocence from her loving heart made her connect with the school socialites, athletes, cheerleaders, and even the self-professed nerds. Sophia would joke that inside every person is a nerd just waiting to be celebrated and she never took life too seriously so as not to laugh at herself.

One of the reasons that Sophia had so many friends is because she had a 'light" within her spirit that drew others to her. She always seemed to have friends around her because of her free spirit put others at ease. In fact, Sophia seemed to have a mission since she was a small child to inspire others and make them like themselves more after having been around her, than they did before they met her. It was her gift to them, and if she could make others feel better about themselves through a kind word, then Sophia was always the one offering that positive word.

Since Sophia was an only child, she enjoyed the company of friends her age and having both parents who worked outside of the home, she learned to occupy her time through reading and writing. Being an exceptional student, Sophia loved to learn and she spent many hours reading books, even though her friends would tease her that books went out in the dinosaur era and she should embrace e-readers and the 21st century. No amount of teasing would take away her love of touching the pages of old books and being able to earmark a page that she was interested in. Sophia drank in the knowledge from these books like water and her favorite were mysteries and new age novels.

Because so much of Sophia's time was spent on homework and reading, the extra time she did have was spent either volunteering with her mom at a local animal shelter, being involved in fundraisers to raise money for various charities, or traveling with her family. Since her dad was often taking business trips and her mom was off in the summers from teaching, they would enjoy traveling with her dad so they could all be together.

Sophia's parents, Joseph and Gracie, were both very successful. Their self-made successes were largely due the live balance they have achieved through working hard and smart. Her dad was an entrepreneur who designed computer software programs to help hospitals run more efficiently and her mom was a successful teacher who developed a passion for writing and went on publishing several successful self-help books.

Due to Joseph and Gracie's schedules, Sophia's parents spent as much time as possible with her. Some teenagers may think too much, but Sophia thought it was the right amount. Her parents believed in preparing Sophia for the world. One of lessons was how to be responsible and make decisions that always have consequences. They created an acronym for Sophia so she would remember easily every time she was faced with a decision no matter how big or small, she would be mature enough to make responsible choices. Sophia knew this as "CDC" as her parents referred to it which stood for Choices, Decisions, and Consequences. Sophia learned that if she was with a group of friends or in a classroom environment and she had a choice to make then she needed to weigh the outcome, make a decision and deal with the consequences. Because of this mindset, Sophia rarely made poor choices that required her to be ashamed of the consequences.

Sophia had a strong connection to Gracie. They talked about dreams of becoming a fashion designer or stylist and her mom would share dreams of writing her first novel that would inspire the world. Some of Sophia's fondest memories were of her and her mom getting to spend time together shopping, eating out, and walking along the beach sharing their inner hopes and dreams. They both loved to laugh, dream, and the memories they created this summer were ones Sophia would never forget. Sophia and her mom would often play a game called "what if," which included scenarios such as what if you were stranded on a dessert island and could have one thing with you then what would you choose? Or other scenarios such as what if you won twenty million dollars in the lottery and had to spend it in one day, then how would you spend it?

Both Sophia and her mom were very good at creating scenes that would force Sophia to step outside of the box with her thinking, as her dad always wanted Sophia to be a leader and not a follower. Her dad encouraged opportunities that would push her to think outside the box and look at the situation through a solutions perspective rather than a reactive perspective. This type of creative thinking enabled Sophia to always be proactive in her life and consider more options to solutions than others around her thought possible.

During their fun mini-vacations as Sophia would call them, she and her mom would people watch and try to create pretend scenarios that they thought others were contending with, and then try to find solutions to their problems. For instance Sophia recalls one afternoon while she and her mom were shopping, that they were watching a young couple arguing in the mall, and even though they were trying to be discreet, they were still being noticed by many. Sophia saw the young girl try to walk away from the situation and her boyfriend grabbed her by the arm and pulled him towards her.

This made several people take notice and wait to ensure the young lady didn't need further assistance. As Sophia and her mom watched and studied their behavior, Sophia's mom asked "What would you do if you were dating a young man who appeared to be controlling and Daddy and I didn't approve of him?" Sophia looked at her mom then back to the young couple who were arguing and she thought for a moment. "I wouldn't date anyone that you and Daddy didn't approve of. First of all, there are choices, decisions, and consequences that are connected to dating someone who was so grabby and bossy, and secondly I don't like people bossing me around – especially not some dumb boy." Sophia's mom smiled and nodded in approval as she turned her attention back to the couple.

"I only hope that one day very soon this young girl realizes her own potential," Gracie continued. "There are many lifelong consequences associated with settling for a relationship with another person who doesn't respect you or themself." One of the many ways Sophia's mom taught her about life lessons was to use experiences that others around them were having, so she could relate them to personal life lessons. As a teacher, Sophia's mom used her gift of teaching not only in the classroom but outside in the real world as well. Sophia was so excited when her mom made a decision to stop teaching and begin writing full-time so she could share her knowledge with the world.

Sophia believed that she got her love of learning through her parents, and since they thirsted for knowledge in everything they did Sophia learned to do the same. Her parents were very in tune with their ability to create success in their careers by creating their own opportunities rather than working for others. Sophia loved the fact that both of her parents treated her like an adult from a very young age and taught her that she can design the life of her dreams through being aware of what she wanted and make goal lists so she could accomplish them one by one.

Although she was only fourteen, Sophia had an undeniable faith in believing what she could not see but felt with her heart and her spirit. "Some things cannot be explained," she would explain to others, "but they just feel right." Behind Sophia's big brown eyes was a young girl who thought like an old soul. She was wise beyond her years and possessed the maturity of a young girl, but her parents would notice moments of reflection and words of wisdom that echoed Sophia's understanding; that there is more to life than what meets the eye. Life was about magical moments and being a part of the process of creating her dreams while learning from those around her. Sophia's wisdom was revealed through her encouraging words to her friends, her intuitive nature, and her ability to know when someone was feeling badly without them uttering a single word.

Sophia took a certain pride in knowing she had a keen sense of perception, and in the moments where she was able to make a friend or stranger feel better about themselves she actually thought that she may want to become a counselor when she grew up. Life was about helping people and if she could help others, it would allow her to feel good about herself while making others feel good about themselves as well. Life has a funny way of working out when you're so young, because there is so much living to do and the world is always open to you. Sophia only wishes now for those moments when the world seemed like it possessed infinite possibilities of happiness and joy. Little did Sophia know that the following months of her life would teach her the power of love and what it meant to truly be alive.

The Diagnosis
Chapter 2

Sophia remembers September 11th like it was yesterday, because it was not only the day that changed the lives of so many people in the terrorist attack at the World Trade Center, but it also represented the day that forever changed Sophia's illusion of perceived comfort and safety within her own family. Just after hearing on the news about the attacks on the World Trade Center, Sophia received some devastating news about the health of her mom. She had sensed a different mood when her mom stopped by to take her home from school. Although everybody was upset about the attacks earlier that day, Sophia couldn't help but think that there was something more to her mom's quiet mood and worried expression. As they were driving home, Sophia noticed her mom staring off into silence and remained quiet all the way home. This wasn't like her at all, as she always started out the trip home asking Sophia about her day and what the highlight and the hardest part of it was. This trip home was very different and suddenly Sophia began worrying that there may be something more that her mom was not telling her.

As they pulled into the driveway, Sophia's mom managed a soft but strained smile and suggested that she go inside to wash up and prepare for dinner. As Sophia leaped out of the car she turned around to notice that her mom was still sitting behind the driver's seat and had not moved toward the door. Instead, she just braced the steering wheel with white knuckles and swallowed hard before dropping her head on the steering wheel. Sophia realized that her mom was crying but she was too afraid to go back to the car to ask her what was wrong, so instead she did as her mother instructed and went into the house to clean up for dinner. As Sophia walked into the door, her father was standing there to meet her and gazed right past her and turned his focus towards her mom who was now getting out of the car slowly. He walked past Sophia and moved quickly towards her mom who was making her way towards them, and as he met her in the driveway he grabbed her by the shoulders and pulled her into his arms.

Something in Sophia's stomach dropped and it felt as if there was a lead weight taking ownership of her stomach. She felt sick and began trembling as she watched them both walk into the house, with her father's arms still wrapped around her mother to bring her comfort. "Sophia," he said in a soft voice, "sit down we have something to tell you." Sophia felt the lump in her throat grow harder and she felt as if she could barely swallow as she sat down on the sofa and watch her mother gently grab her small hands. "Sophia," her mother said, "I just returned from the doctor and I..." suddenly her voice broke and she began to cry. "Sophia, I have breast cancer." These words created such a feeling of fear in Sophia that her cheeks suddenly grew hot and she felt as if she were going to cry, but instead she just sat there and didn't move.

As Sophia's mother and father proceeded to inform her about her diagnosis, Sophia barely moved. Gracie's cancer was in its fourth stage which meant her cancer had spread from her breast to other areas of her body and was inoperable. Her treatment would be difficult which would include chemotherapy and radiation. The side-effects of the treatments would make her feel terrible and it would most likely make her lose her hair. As they shared with her this devastating information, her parents were careful to speak slowly and explain everything to her as if she were an adult – not a young teenager. This helped Sophia because although she was young, she was also a smart girl and appreciated her parents treating her as such. The more her parents explained the illness and treatment the more questions Sophia had. "Is mom going to be alright? Will the treatments take all of the cancer away? Why did mom get sick?" ...and as the answers to her questions were being responded to, Sophia suddenly got a sick feeling in her stomach and uttered the words..."is mom going to die?"

The startled reaction from her parents caused Sophia to stop asking questions and just stare at them both in silence. "No Sophia," her mom whispered as she slowly shook her head, "I am not going to die...we are going to fight this!" Silence permeated the room and all Sophia could hear was the beating of her own heartbeat as it beat so hard, she could swear that her shirt was moving. This was too much for her to take, and Sophia jumped to her feet and ran upstairs into her room, slammed the door behind her, and threw herself on the bed. As she sobbed face down into her pink comforter, Sophia felt the stress of the last five minutes overtake her body and all she could do was cry. "How could this happen?" she thought, and in the silence of her room Sophia cried herself to sleep.

When she awoke, Sophia felt the tender hand of her mom stroking her hair and felt her lying down on the bed next to her. As she pulled her tear-stained face up to her mom, she wanted to begin crying all over again but the tears wouldn't come. She just buried her face next to her mom's shoulder and felt the last of the tears fall gently down her cheeks. "Momma?" Sophia choked the words out slowly, "are you going to be ok?" Just then she felt the arms of her mother pull her closer into her embrace and cradled her back and forth. "Yes Sophia," her mom replied, "I am going to be just fine and we will get through this together as a family." Sophia looked up to study her mom's face and noticed that she had been crying as well. Her mom smiled down at Sophia and said to her, "I'm not going anywhere, because you are my world and I will always be by your side."

Sophia closed her eyes and allowed herself to be cradled in the arms of her mother. There was a comfort that only her mom could provide her and all it took was the touch of her hand to warm her spirit. Sophia was always connected to her mom and she didn't even have to touch her for Sophia to sense her energy and know she was there. For years, Sophia would play games with her mom and close her eyes, and have her mom walk towards her and Sophia would tell her when she sensed her energy around her. The games grew more exciting when Sophia could feel the warmth of her energy when her mom was not close enough to touch her. All it took was sensing her presence around her, and Sophia knew when she walked into a room without even looking up to see if it was her. This was a connection that Sophia's mom enjoyed as well because she wanted to feel the warmth of an emotional and now physical connection to her daughter. Only now the connection became stronger and the fear of losing her mom was even more terrifying than ever.

Sophia's mom pulled back her long, brown hair from her face and looked into her eyes and just studied her for a moment. Finally she said, "Sophia I want you to ask me anything you want to and I promise you that the questions that I don't know the answer to, I will research it until I do. Knowledge is power and the more information we have about dealing with this disease, the more empowered we will feel, and the stronger we will become." Sophia looked into her mom's eyes, the same eyes that expressed joy and pride towards her good grades just a few days ago, and they appeared worried and swollen from crying. There was something in her gaze back to Sophia that made her appear frightened and unsure of the future, but her mom was right about one thing. Sophia was going to help her mom through this cancer and together as a family, they will beat this disease – she just knew it.

Gracie had been going to her treatments for months with Sophia and Joseph at her side. As the weeks and months passed, Sophia watched as the disease slowly progressed and the light that once shined in her mom's eyes was now beginning to dim. Her face grew weary and the eyes that had once sparkled were now growing dim and tired. Sophia refused to acknowledge in her mind what her heart already knew – that the cancer was beginning to overtake her mom's once healthy body. As the disease progressed, Sophia dealt with the emotions of it all by immersing herself in reading, writing, and sewing clothes.

Sophia could not understand the severity of the cancer until one day when she least expected it… Sophia's mom collapsed. They rushed her to the hospital but by the time the ambulance arrived at the hospital, it was too late. Sophia stood frozen in the hospital emergency room waiting area as the doctor put his hand on Sophia's dad's shoulders and spoke in a very low voice to him. Joseph's shoulders dropped, his head fell into his hands as Sophia watched his complexion turned pale and he began shaking his head. "I'm sorry," she overheard the doctor say as he stood up and nodded to Sophia as he exited the waiting room.

"Daddy?" Sophia cried as she watched her usually strong father crumble to the chair and began to weep. She ran to him and threw her arms around his shoulders and together they cried and held each other tightly while the realization of her mom's death began to permeate into every fiber of her being. Sophia was terrified for herself and for her dad, and the powerful feeling of loneliness and isolation shook her once secure world.

How were they going to make it through without the love of her mom? After all, she was the glue that held the family together and the more Sophia attempted to understand the reality of her world caving in, the worse she felt. "Please momma," Sophia cried, "please don't leave us." As Sophia closed eyes tightly in any attempt to escape the rush of fear that overwhelmed her, all she could hear were their cries echoing in the silence of the hospital waiting room.

Saying Good-Bye
Chapter 3

Across town in a small church Pastor Abraham sat motionless and alone in a small corner of one of the pews as he stared at the wooden casket that laid in front of him. The polished wood reflected the light of the dimly lit room which made the church feel even smaller. As his eyes studied the closed casket, the Pastor's attention turned to the white roses and lilies that cascaded down the sides of the wooden box that held the precious body of one of his congregation. Gracie was nearly a daughter to Pastor Abraham as he had known her entire family since she was a little girl. Gracie's love of both white lilies and roses was evident as she asked for her casket be covered in wreaths that surrounded it was covered with the beautiful flowers of all shapes and colors from white roses to calla lilies to white trumpet Easter lilies that blanketed the box and gave it a sense of warmth and comfort.

Next to Pastor Abraham sat a young girl dressed in a demure black dress with a simple lace collar. At first glance one would have thought she was prepared for Sunday school as she appeared very comfortable in her attire while her legs nervously swayed back and forth. As her fingers anxiously traced the string of tiny white pearls around her neck, Sophia could not bear to look up at the casket that lay in front of her. She swallowed hard to keep the tears from streaming down her face and it seemed that the harder she fought the tears, the more they wanted to flow down her rosy cheeks.

On her lap rested one single red rose that filled the air with the scent that once represented joy and love. Now it signified the emotions of despair and hopelessness, and there was nothing Sophia could do to escape them. As she prayed for relief from the pain that clutched her heart, all Sophia could think about was how embarrassed she was that she was the only person who brought a rose to her mom's funeral. As her attention shifted from the polka dots on her dress to the rose on her lap, she felt Pastor Abraham's hand rest on hers. "Sophia," he whispered. She could not bear to lift her head and look at him, so her gaze remained on her lap as she heard his voice once again. "I know you are hurting, and I cannot say anything to you that will bring you comfort...but I pray that I will be able to allow God to speak through me to give you peace."

Slowly Sophia looked up to catch his gaze and as Pastor Abraham rose to his feet, Sophia noticed his tall stature overpowered her small frame. She wanted to respond to him but words were too difficult to speak, and her emotions were so heavy that not even her thoughts could create a safety net from her grief. As Sophia's gaze met Pastor Abraham's, her eyes caught the flicker of his gray eyes staring back at her and as he turned to walk to the pulpit she noticed a slight smile cross his thin lips as he winked at her. Turning away from her gaze, Pastor Abraham walked in a slightly awkward gait but his demeanor gave the impression of confidence and courage.

As Pastor Abraham stood before the pulpit his tall and lanky body overpowered the slightly undersized and fragile stand that stood in front of him. He closed his eyes, took in a deep breath, and slowly exhaled before the church echoed the sound of his deep voice. "There is a saying that I have lived my life by," he proceeded as he looked out into the large crowd of mourners that had poured into the church. "Where there is love, there is God, and I have no doubt that God has filled the room with His Angels to bring you comfort in this time of grief." Pastor Abraham's eyes gazed back at Sophia who remained fixed on the casket that lay in front of her. *Father, please speak through me because I don't know what to say to bring her peace.* His prayer sent a sudden chill through the Pastor's body and he knew that God heard him and was with him.

"Today we have to lie to rest a beautiful child of God who once graced the world with her love and light. She was aptly named Grace because her mother and I saw something very special in her eyes when she was born. You see Gracie was the light of our lives, but she also served to light the lives of so many around her and each and every one of you was once touched by her light." As his eyes scanned the room of mourners, Pastor Abraham's hands began to shake and his lip began to quiver. "Today I have to relinquish my daughter into the hands of God where she can continue lighting the lives of each one of us without restriction from a body that became ill. Today I have to explain to a young girl whose relationship with her momma was cut too short, why she has to say good-bye to the one person who has been connected to her since her inception in the womb. I also have to explain to this young girl that despite her sorrow and grief, God heard her words of pleading and chose to take her momma home to be with Him once again."

Sophia closed her eyes tightly to avoid any tears from streaming down her face. She promised herself that she would be strong and not cry, but more than the tears she was fighting, her anger and resentment towards God at this very moment was too much to bear. Especially when a man was standing in front of her thinking he was going to convince her that God was as real and loving as she once thought he was. Pastor Abraham continued, "Cancer is a terrible disease but it never defined Gracie, because she knew what defined her were her thoughts, her emotions, and her actions. This is why this church is overflowing with people who loved her and were connected to her in some beautiful way. I want to share with you a story that I shared with Gracie when we found out that she was sick and her body was fighting this disease." Sophia's eyes began to open slowly and she looked down at her feet as she listened quietly to Pastor Abraham.

"There was once a little girl who danced with Angels near the gates of heaven, and every day she would try to peek through the silver gates as she wondered what was on the other side. Father, she would ask, when can I open the gates and play on the other side? She would ask, and every day she was given the same answer...you must wait my child because you are not ready to play on that side yet. As her big beautiful eyes stared through the brilliant gate, she would reach out her hand through the gate as if trying to reach something magical on the other side. But why can't I go play now? Why do I have to wait? What's out there? The more she was told that she was not ready to play on that side of the gate, the more inquisitive she became. One bright shiny day she ran over to the gate once more and before asking her usual question of when she could play, the little girl looked up at her Father and asked the right question...what can I do to get to play on that side of the gate?

As her Father smiled down at her, he gently scooped her up and sat her on his lap. 'My child there is much beauty on the other side of the gate, but there is also a great deal of pain as well. On this side you know love, joy, peace, and everything is possible and beautiful. On the other side of the gate, you will forget much of what you know and your journey on that side is to remember all of these beautiful things that you are experiencing here right now. Souls travel to the other side of the gate because they want to discover more about their own greatness, but in the process of discovering your greater self you forget how amazing you already are. It is a trade-off but a large sacrifice that is not to be taken lightly, because in order to discover your greatness and continue transforming into a greater version of yourself you must experience who you are *not.*' The little girl stared up at her Father and looked quizzically at him as she attempted to understand what he was trying to

30

say to her. 'On the other side of this gate,' her Father proceeded to explain 'is a journey that will begin with you learning how to work your body because it is much different here. You have no limits, no pain, and no fear but on the other side of the gate you learn to experience all of these emotions. You begin to work with a physical body from the moment of your re-birth and you must learn how to work with this physical body in order to experience your journey. But you are not your physical body my child, you are still very much a perfect soul that is just using a physical experience to grow into a greater version of yourself. Through this body you will experience physical and emotional pain but you will also experience great joy and love.'

The little girl studied her Father as he spoke and finally broke her silence as she asked, "What will happen during these times of pain?" As he smiled down at her, the Father replied, "You will reach out to me for comfort and solace and I will be as present there as I am here right this very moment except you won't be able to see me as you do now. You will only be able to feel me and hear me, but this often causes confusion because many souls choose not to remember me in their journey. For those who forget me, I am still very much present in their experience but through their forgetting me they often feel alone. Across this gate my child is a journey that allows you to experience yourself as a co-creator with me. Since you and I are one just as we are right now, you get to experience creating your journey with me with the only difference being that you cannot see me as you do now. But the lack of awareness of me combined with the experiences of emotions that are sometimes painful can lead a soul to undergo their journey in great sorrow.'

The little girl listened intently as she processed the message and carefully asked, 'what if I were to go to the other side of the gate to play and I forget you?' She heard a chuckle and saw her Father smile down at her, 'I will never let you forget me my child because you and I are forever connected with or without your awareness of me. I will remind you that although you cannot see me, you can feel my presence in your soul and you can hear my words as I whisper them into your heart. We will have a beautiful relationship that is so personal to you that only you and I will experience our communication through prayer. I will lead you to experience great joy and amidst your moments of sorrow I will remind you that the emotions of fear will pass and I am ever present with you.'

As the little girl wondered why anyone would choose to experience fear, she asked, 'but Father, why then would anyone want to go to the other side of the gate to play?' As soon as she asked the question, she realized that her soul had a longing to experience playing on the other side. 'What kind of games do they have on the other side of the gate?' she asked. 'There are many games to play on the other side my child, as there are games of love, joy peace, and abundance. There are also games of teaching other souls to reconnect with me through tolerance, forgiveness, empowerment, and inspiration. You get to select the game you want to experience and have it be as long or as short lived as you choose. Whatever happens though, you will always come back to this side of the gate when you are ready and I will be here waiting for you to see me again. A smile curled up at the tips of the little girl's mouth and she expressed interest in wanting to play on the other side of the gate.

'What game do you wish to experience my child?' her Father asked. The little girl pondered the question and then slowly replied, 'I want to play with my best friend on the other side of the gate. I wish to experience playing with her and getting to be with her every day of my journey there. I would love to remind her that she is loved by you and I want to remind her that you are real when she has moments of forgetting. On the other side of the gate, I want to inspire her through my own actions and then maybe we can come back together,' the little girl responded. 'What if your best friend isn't ready to come back to this side of the gate when you are?' the father asked. 'What if she wants to play on that side a little longer than you do? Are you ready to leave her and come back early without her?'

The little girl thought about the question and replied, "yes, so I can stay connected to her on this side of the gate just like you do!' The Father smiled in agreement and said, 'how will you leave your friend? Do you want to come back to this side of the gate suddenly or do you want to have time to say good-bye?' The little girl sat up and looked her Father in the eyes, "I have to be able to say good-bye to her because I would want to be sure she remembered that you and I will still be there for her except she just won't be able to see me. I would want to remind her that the other side of the gate is just an illusion and that those experiences don't define her but just teach her about becoming a greater version of herself. Most importantly I want to be able to touch her and love her and say goodbye to her so she doesn't miss me as much when I come back here. Can I do all of those things on the other side of the gate?'

'Yes my child,' the Father responded, 'you can do anything you want through the experiences you choose. Is there anything else you want to experience on this journey?' The little girl sat back on her Father's lap and rested her head on his shoulder. "I want to experience love in the way that you love me. I want to know what it feels like to love me unconditionally, and to be patient with me, speak kindly to me, and want to see me experience joy the way you are towards me. How can I do that?' As she looked up at her Father, she saw a twinkle in His eyes and his love was beyond words – only feelings. 'I will give you a body that will allow you to take care of yourself and love yourself the way I love you. I will grant you experiences that honor your body and your soul and as you remember that the other side of the gate is a temporary illusion, your body will not last forever but only as long as you desire your experience to last.'

The little girl listened and pondered this for a few moments, 'what if I forget you?' Just then her Father sat her up and pulled her towards him. 'How do you want me to remind you that I am in your heart and by your side when you forget me?' Just then the little girl's eyes caught sight of a bright, beautiful, red rose. 'I want you to let me feel you, hear you in my soul, and when all else fails, send me roses from heaven so I remember that this is the sign I asked of you before I crossed over to the other side of the gate. I won't share this with anybody so I know that it is our secret on the other side of the gate.' The Father gazed lovingly into his daughter's eyes and said, 'you are ready, go to the other side of the gate and play. I want you to remember that whatever happens know I am only a thought away. I love you forever."

Experiencing Grief

Chapter 4

The weeks that followed the death of Sophia's mom was almost unbearable, and nobody could have prepared her for the amount of pain on a physical and emotional level that one experiences when they grieve. For months, light would hurt Sophia's eyes and loud, sharp sounds would pierce through her soul – feeling as if they were cutting her in half. She would walk numbly throughout the day feeling completely unattached to anyone or anything, and all she wanted to do was sleep. The heaviness that her soul felt was almost incomprehensible and although she had always been a strong spiritual person, Sophia stopped praying.

Faith was one of those gifts that had come and gone with her mom's passing and Sophia felt betrayed by God and alone in her faith. It felt as if she was looking into a mirror and the only reflection she saw staring back at her was darkness. It was as if she stopped existing and in her own eyes, Sophia felt like she did stop existing the moment of her momma's passing. She spent all of her energy trying to get through the days so she could go home and go to sleep until this nightmare passed.

It wouldn't be for many more months that the pain in her heart began to slowly heal, and although she was still terribly sad Sophia began to find joy in the small blessings that surrounded her. Piece by piece she noticed life in the small miracles every day from smiling at a joke her friend would say or giggling at the burnt pancakes that her father tried so desperately to make like her momma used to. As time moved forward, so did the healing process until one day Sophia realized that she could get throughout the entire day without crying and without the immense pain in her heart.

As Sophia's heart began to slowly mend, she was able to start sleeping better again because that was something she lost after her mom passed away. Sophia would lie awake at night and recall all of the moments she could just so she didn't risk forgetting her mom. Her greatest fear was that as her heart healed, she would forget her mom and she didn't want to risk forgetting anything about her. Not the way she combed her hair, the way she smelled of her favorite perfume, or the way her touch felt when she kissed her cheek. All of the things Sophia once took for granted became gifts that she feared would be forgotten.

As the nights progressed that year, Sophia found it easier to sleep for even moments and although she would have many restless nights, Sophia found comfort in lying awake at nights and remembering her mom's voice, laughter, mannerisms, and anything that would keep her "alive" in her thoughts. Sophia found that during the times where she was acutely aware of her broken heart she would recall the most detailed characteristics of her mom until through the combination of memory and grief, Sophia would find herself immersed in the feeling of having her momma's energy around her. There would be nights where Sophia would convince herself of the illusion that her momma was still with her even though she couldn't see her. At least she believed it was an illusion...or was it?

As the weeks passed Sophia's heart ache was not as strong as it was before, she began learning how to breathe once again. It's interesting how time manages to turn pain into numbness and throughout the journey of grief Sophia learned how to do just that...numb her pain.

Even though her desire to hang out with her friends had slowly turned into her need to be alone, Sophia found comfort in solitude, and what once brought her joy in making others laugh turned into a struggle just to speak to her father and closest relatives. No longer was she the energetic young girl that sparked conversation with strangers, now Sophia was the quiet girl in the corner who was just trying to disappear through her silence. The bright colors of clothing that once adorned her tiny frame remained tucked away in the closet where the hopes and dreams of one day becoming a designer were also placed. Day by day and week by week Sophia was disappearing and being replaced by sorrow and depression.

The one person who remained closest to her was Sophia's dad Joe, and he was trying desperately to deal with his own sorrow from losing the only love of his life that he had known since high school. Everyday Joe would struggle to make conversation with his daughter who so often had to be silenced because she spoke too much during dinner, television movies, and at church. Now the effort came in just getting her to speak at all, and once he made the decision to have Sophia meet with a grief counselor her silence transferred from home into that counselor's office. She couldn't speak the words or process the emotions that broke her heart and her spirit let alone allow a stranger into her dark world.

Joe knew that with time she would eventually begin to heal but how he wished that the time would hurry because there was nothing he could do to comfort his beautiful daughter. One night as he walked past Sophia's room, he heard her cries and once again as he reached for the door to hold her as he had done so many nights before something stopped him. Tonight he needed to allow Sophia the space to grieve, breathe, and be alone in her own thoughts so she could begin processing them without his interruption. Tonight he decided to go into his own room and allow his daughter the chance to process this terrible loss on her own terms and check in on her again in a few minutes.

As Joe lay his head down on the pillow, he could feel hot tears streaming down his cheeks. *How am I going to do this without you Gracie?* He thought, as the realization of his wife's passing became more real. *I don't know what I'm doing... I can't comfort her the way you did...dear God, what am I going to do?* As he rolled over to bury his head in his pillow, Joe heard the crackle of paper underneath his head. As he lifted the pillow his gaze fell on a small pink envelope with the words *To My Dearest Joseph* written on the front. The envelope appeared as though it had been neatly placed underneath his pillow just moments ago because the letter had no creases on it and the perfection in which it laid made Joseph wonder how long it had actually been there. As he carefully picked up the letter, Joseph slowly opened the envelope and read the words that had been hand written by his late bride.

My Dearest Joseph,

As you read these words my heart goes out to you as I know you are dealing with the sorrow of my passing. I want you to know that I fought a hard battle and what may appear as my loss was in fact my victory. You see cancer is a terrible disease and as you have witnessed, its toxic effects overtake a person's body and destroy it from the inside out. What so many fail to see as they watch this overtake and destroy their loved ones lives is the fact that cancer is also one opportunity to buy time to love. It is a horrible disease and creates pain on both emotional and physical levels for those affected by it and I suffered terribly from this fight. I also received the gift of time to be with you and Sophia and build a life of love and purity during my fight.

Many people who cross over are not allowed the opportunity of time, and don't get to say their "I love you's" and their "goodbye's." One of the blessings I received from battling this disease was the gift of time with you and Sophia, and we got to share words, love, and joy that many don't receive. We got to create memories and share our love for one another knowing that I would not be around much longer and for that you should be very grateful... I am. I was able to realize through my pain that I would not be around to help you raise Sophia, and I was blessed with time to share my words with her that I would not have been afforded had I crossed over instantly without time for suffering.

Accompanying this letter is a pink envelope with Sophia's name written on it. I would like for you to give this letter to her now. It is important and I am so thankful that out of all the people in this world, I got to share my love and my life with you. Most importantly I am grateful to God that I have left her in the most perfect hands to raise her – yours. I know this is difficult Joseph, but know that you are never alone. Think of me and I will be there for you.

I love you forever,

Gracie

The Connection
Chapter 5

As Joseph studied at the hand-written letter, the shock began to leave his body as his once white face began to fill with color, and the surprise of finding this letter began to sink into his heart. Although it seemed impossible that he found the letter under his pillow on this particular evening, Joseph believed in the impossible and right now he needed to get this letter into Sophia's hands. Somehow he had managed to sleep on that letter for weeks after his wife's death and just in time when he knew his daughter needed a miracle and a piece of hope in her heart, Joseph discovers the letter completely uncompromised and in perfect condition under his pillow. How had he not found it before tonight?

The more Joseph thought about the letter, the more he questioned his sanity and most importantly, how he was going to explain this to Sophia. Although her letter was in the pink stationary that Gracie loved so much, and it was her handwriting on the letter, Joseph didn't know what to believe. But he did know this much – this letter was written for Sophia by her mother and Joseph was going to deliver it to her in the manner in which it was intended...through faith. As Joseph clutched the pink envelope in his hands, he brought it close to his face and inhaled the scent of Gracie's favorite flower. He never understood how she managed to smell so beautiful, but the scent of roses was lingering on Sophia's letter. How was that possible when he had been lying on this letter for weeks before discovering it and did not even smell the familiar scent that reminded him of Grace since they began dating in High School?

As these questions filled Joseph's mind, he picked up the delicate pink envelop and smelled it one last time. The fragrance lingered in the air as the memories of Grace in her healthiest state crossed his mind while the reel played back as he remembered her discovering a small lump in her breast, which turned into a nightmare of months of chemotherapy, radiation, surgery, and ultimately her passing. How it turned from a small lump into her passing within one year was still so sudden for Joseph that he could not even imagine how difficult it was for his beautiful daughter right now. What he did understand was the importance of delivering this letter to Sophia this very moment and allowing the magic of the moment to heal her tears...even if for 10 minutes.

As Joseph hurried down the hall towards Sophia's room, he began experiencing feelings of joy, hope, fear, and uncertainty. How would he explain this to Sophia if she did not respond in a positive manner to the letter? Right now, the need to bring comfort to his daughter overcame the need to self-preserve so as he watched his trembling hands reach for Sophia's bedroom door, he silently prayed and asked God to bless his daughter as she received this gift from heaven. "Sophia...?"He heard his strained voice crack in the stillness of the dark room..."are you awake?" Fearing frightening her, Joseph slowly moved towards Sophia's bed and heard her rustle in the dark. "Daddy?" Sophia said. *She's awake... thank you God,* he prayed as his fingers turned the switch of her night table lamp.

As the light came on Joseph stared at the beautiful face that stared at him in the dimly lit room. Sophia resembled her mom in so many ways that he realized for the first time since her passing, that it scared him. Sophia's eyes were the eyes of Gracie staring back at him through a child and her mannerisms were so much like her mom's that it terrified him. How would he have the strength and courage to see Sophia every day and not feel fear that he would lose her too? Despite his fear, Joseph knew that this letter was a gift to his daughter and whatever it contained was in fact written by her mother and delivered at a time in her grieving process when she needed hope the most. This was his gift to her tonight... even if it was for one night of allowing Sophia the comfort of a good night's sleep, he was going to deliver the letter first and deal with the questions afterwards.

"Sophia?..." he heard his own whispering voice, and said a quick prayer before he handed her the letter.... As Sophia reached for the pink envelope, Joseph noticed her hand shaking just as his had done moments before. Her large brown eyes stared intently at the pink envelope and a smile crept across his lips as he watched her smell the pink envelope for the all familiar scent of Grace. Sophia held the envelope close to her heart and looked up at Joseph with the most questioning eyes...., "Daddy?" she said as she stared at him for any kind of logical explanation to which he offered none. "I found it... underneath my pillow tonight Sophia."

Even as he heard his own voice explaining it, this whole thing still made no sense to him. He looked back at Sophia with the same eyes that reflected anticipation....*open it,* he thought but he understood that she needed time to process this. His only hope was that she would not wait until the morning to read it, and as prayers would answer him, Joseph watched his precious daughter slowly open a letter that was written by and delivered to her late mother in just the perfect time when she needed it most. *Thank you God*, he thought as he watched her open the letter and stared at her intently as she read the letter aloud...

My Dearest Sophia,

You are reading this letter so you may find comfort in the grief you are experiencing from my passing. I have watched you grow and spread your joy and radiant light to share love in all that you do. Now I see you struggle through your grief, and that light that used to shine from your spirit is slowly becoming dim from your sorrow and heartache. How can a child go through something so profound without the slightest understanding of life and death, yet here you are. At your young age you had to endure watching me battle a disease that destroyed my body as well as your faith. With every passing day, I saw the light dim in your eyes until you came to the realization that I was losing the battle against cancer. Sophia I need you to know that although cancer destroyed my body, it did not destroy my soul and even though you can no longer see me in the physical form as you have known me, I am still very much alive.

Sophia, I need you to understand that before you continue reading this letter because I am going to call on every bit of truth that your soul knows but has yet to understand. You have relied on what you can see with your eyes in order to believe that it exists and now I am asking you to believe that which you do not see and know that it also exists. Remember when you began praying as a small child, and every night before you went to sleep you would kneel by your bedside and pray to God. There were many nights when you asked me how I knew that God heard your prayers, and my response was always the same..."have faith Sophia Rose; God hears your every thought and word."

Now I am asking you to have the same faith to ask your heart and soul to believe that which it already knows to be truth, but your mind has yet to understand. I am here with you and even though you can no longer see or feel me, have faith that you have not lost me forever. You witnessed my passing away and now are experiencing my rebirth into the non-physical form. This letter serves to help aide you through your painful journey through the cycle of grief, and although your Daddy loves you very much, not even he can alleviate your pain. I know you are enduring an emotional agony that nobody can comfort, but somehow I believe this letter may help bring you that relief in the smallest and yet most miraculous way.

I cannot tell you how sorry I am that you had to watch me endure the painful journey of experiencing cancer, as you witnessed this disease attack my body and slowly destroy it cell by cell. You witnessed the fear in my eyes and the pain in my heart as we visited doctor after doctor just looking for anyone to tell us that everything was going to be alright... but it wasn't. As the disease progressed, you saw how it took a toll on my body and as the strength left my body it never left my soul. What you didn't see was the fight that my spirit held throughout this entire ordeal, and the days I battled my body just to remain near you and Daddy.

My spirit refused to be defeated and although my body was losing the battle, I won the war. You see my dearest Sophia, this disease bought me the most precious gift I could have received knowing that I would be leaving you...it bought me the gift of time. But this gift did not come without a sacrifice and that was one I was willing to make. I got to watch you grow for an extra 6 months, and I looked forward to seeing you come home at the end of the day just so you could sit on my bed and tell me about your day.

This disease never got to take away the moments I met your eyes and held you in my arms, just for another second to stroke your beautiful long hair. You saw the pain in my body but what you didn't see was the joy in my heart when I got to touch your delicate skin one more day. What you didn't see was the gratitude in my heart when I got to listen to the sounds of your breathing as you lay next to me and slept. Cancer was a horrible disease my beautiful child, but it bought me time to turn something horrible into a gift that allowed me to cherish moments that I once took for granted. How many souls can say they exited their journey through life in an attitude of gratitude?

I know this is a lot to take in and I understand if you may need time to process this letter, but know that this letter is as real as I still am. I understand that you have so many questions and are using your strength just to get through the days, but know that as time goes by you will heal from the ache that your heart is enduring. Meanwhile, I am sending you letters to guide you through this journey of grief so you will understand the transition I have made from life in the physical form to life in the spiritual form. My love for you transcends time and space and although you do not understand this now, you will help many after your own tiny soul has healed from this journey.

I am going to provide you an opportunity to understand the truth about life, love, and growing beyond the most painful experiences of your life. You are forever a part of me my beautiful child, and from your root of life to my heart will you heal slowly from the loss of my role in your life. I am still your mother now and forever and will love you forever. Know this and your heart will take solace in the comfort of this truth tonight. As for the remainder of this letter, I would like for you to tuck it underneath your pillow and read it in the morning when you have a fresh mind and an awakened heart.

I love you forever,

Momma

Everything is an Illusion
Chapter 6

As the sunlight filled the room, Sophia awoke from a full night's sleep that she had not experienced since her mom passed away. Her long lashes cast a shadow on her cheeks as she opened her eyes and tried to make sense of a dream she had that night about her mom; a beautiful dream that her mom had visited her and sent her a message from a letter in a beautiful pink envelope. As Sophia pushed herself up from her pillow, she felt something in her hand that caught her attention. As she removed her right hand from underneath her pillow Sophia saw the beautiful pink envelope that she had dreamt about just hours before she awoke.

Slowly she opened the letter and continued reading the words that she began the night before. So many thoughts rushed through her head as her heart swelled with emotions of excitement, confusion, and anticipation. It felt as if her mom was alive once again and for a slight moment, the thought of a miracle crossed Sophia's mind. As she focused on the words written by her mom's handwriting, Sophia felt a warmth envelope her body like a blanket, and to her surprise she smelled the scent of a rose. A smile crossed her lips as Sophia recalled sitting next to her mom one evening after a rough chemo treatment, as she explained to her why she named her Sophia Rose. Her favorite actress was Sophia Lauren and she absolutely loved the scent of roses. *"Roses are a beautiful sign of love. Whether it is given to someone in a relationship to tell them I love you, or blessing someone with a gesture of friendship, roses are the universal language of love....and the smell of them brings a smile to my face.*

As Sophia remembered this story she began very thoughtfully reading the letter. Her hands were trembling and tears began filling her eyes which made it even more difficult to read. Slowly Sophia wiped the tears from her eyes, leaned back on her pillow, and continued reading the letter.

My Dearest Sophia,

Now that you have slept and awakened with the realization that you are not dreaming, I want to ensure you understand how much I love you. Nothing will ever separate the love I have for you, not in life and not even in death. You are so young but your soul is more grown than you are even aware, and having to experience my illness and my passing is something I am so sorry you had to endure and so proud of you for your strength and courage. I know you are hurting and since I cannot be there in physical form for you, especially during this painful time of grieving, then I wanted to let you know that I am only a thought away. There is so much that I wanted to share with you but our time in the physical form was cut short from the cancer, but although it stole our time together it did not steal our connection.

There is still so much to teach you and even though I am not there in physical form, I am with you in spirit and want to teach you things that you won't learn in school but is such an important key to having a happy and successful life. Read these words with an open mind and believe them with an open heart. I only wish that I could have been there to see you go to your first dance, stand in the crowd with pride during your graduation, and watch you get married and start a family of your own someday. But what I can do is so much more priceless my beautiful child, because I can teach you the truth about your life and how you can create the experiences of love and truth rather than fear and doubt.

Even though our lives seem worlds apart right now, I am more connected to you than I was when I was in physical form because there is no separation from our energy other than your perception of separation. I only share this knowledge because in order for you to understand what I want to teach you, your mind must remain open to the idea that you may not be able to see me but I am very much alive. I am sending you messages in the only way that we have shared them before so it does not feel so foreign to you. These lessons will bring you to a higher awareness of God, love, and the truth about your experience of life. I love you with all of my heart and forever remain proud that you were my greatest accomplishment.

Everything is an Illusion

Everything is an illusion. God is real, Jesus is real, and the love that you have with the souls around you is real, but everything you see around you is created from an illusion that the emotions, thoughts, and actions of love and fear created. By this I mean that once my soul traveled out of my body in the form that you called death, it became free once again. I am still very much alive through my spirit because I was never my body but always my spirit. Let me see how I can explain this without freaking you out too much....

Oh yes! Remember when you and I played the energy game together, and we held our hands close to one another without actually touching each other? You closed your eyes and could feel my presence even though you did not see me. Whenever I moved my hands closer or farther away from you, you could feel the vibration of the energy and you could sense my energy near you even though I was on the other side of the room? Your mind tricked you into believing an illusion that I wasn't anywhere near you because my body was on the other side of the room but the reality remained that you felt a very real presence around you. This concept is the same thing when it comes to the death of the physical body. Even though you cannot see my body as you knew it before, only means that my energy is still present and by focusing on me then you will begin to sense my energy near you. How do you explain this? Because what we focus our energy on expands, so even though I was not anywhere near you, the act of focusing your attention on me suddenly made me feel closer to you than before.

We are all created from energy which cannot be destroyed, it only changes form. When a person's body cannot sustain itself anymore it dies, but the spirit within the body does not die, it merely transitions and continues living as pure energy. This is what happened to me when my body could not continue fighting the cancer, as the disease destroyed my physical body but it could not destroy my spirit because I like you am created from energy. As pure energy, we all have the ability to communicate but without the physical body being present. Just because I am not standing in front of you speaking through my physical mouth, means that the mind and spirit that I used to create the words I spoke to you with are still very much alive. My physical body is not, so now I connect with you through my thoughts and emotions. Rather than calling you on the telephone, I am able to speak to you through my energy and I still feel the same to you energetically as I did when I was alive in physical form. Now I can come to you in dreams and thoughts rather than through phone and email.

You are all spirit beings having a human experience, not the other way around. As co-creators with God, we are all continually creating through our thoughts, emotions, and actions but everything we focus on is not necessarily reality. You *can focus your thoughts, emotions, and actions to create goals in your life and by dedicating your time to focus your energy on specific things, you create the experience of those things. If you spend your time creating joy, love, and a life of contribution then you will experience the love of the energy you created. On the other hand, if you dedicate your energy and focus to creating negativity, fear, and conflict then you will experience those as well. The most important aspect is to know what you are deliberately creating and be sure that the experience serves you.*

Remember when you came home from school crying because your best friend Ashley was gossiping about you and you had no idea why she was doing something so hurtful to you? Rather than talking to her and resolving the issue, you reacted by not talking to her the entire week, which got her upset with you and she uninvited you to her sleep-over? Finally after myself and her mom got involved, you learned that she never said anything negative about you in the first place, and what you overheard was actually her defending you to another who was trying to gossip about you. Your actions and reactions created an illusion that seemed very real to you and Ashley but the illusion was created nonetheless. The reality was that nothing bad about you was being said by Ashley, but you focusing your energy and creating the illusion of it finally caused a ripple effect of more illusions to be created.

This is what I mean when I tell you that everything is an illusion and just as you create illusions of fear through your thoughts, emotions, and actions, you have the ability to create love which connects you to your reality. So much of what happens in the world around you is an illusion but many souls are feeding it through fear that it continues to expand until it becomes the illusion created by many and then becomes the reality of the masses. Now there are some very terrible experiences that people endure in their lives that have nothing to do with them creating it. By this I mean that some people are victims of crimes, destruction, or much pain from circumstances outside of their control, and these are very real experiences. These events can destroy a person's life and in those moments when terrible things happen to people, there are countless stories of these same souls rising above the trauma to create love, contribution, and much good in the world because they chose to shift their energy from the trauma to allowing Gods love to heal and guide them to joy once again.

They could have chosen to continue living their experiences of trauma over and over again in their lives until they convinced themselves that they cannot experience love and healing. But instead so many souls allow the light and love of God to heal their pain and begin to focus creating experiences of love that is under their control once again. This only shows you the power of the spirit that can endure such pain and heartache, and have the ability to transform their lives into creating experiences of love and joy. You are among these souls Sophia because you have endured a tragic loss that shook the foundation of everything you knew. Losing a loved one is such a traumatic experience and as you are aware when enduring that experience, there feels as if nothing can.

I love you forever,

Momma

God is Real
Chapter 7

As Pastor Abraham's eyes gazed over the crowd, many of who were wiping their eyes and touching their noses with tissues, he took a deep breath. "You see, God knows our deepest fears and desires, but he also honors the journey that each of us took as we all have crossed over the other side of the gate to play and experience a greater version of ourselves. Gracie's journey was completed and she wanted time to tell her best friend that she loved her and wanted to remind her before she left that she would be sitting on her Father's lap sending roses from heaven."

Sophia Rose looked up at Pastor Abraham and smiled. Her long lashes clumped together from the tears that were now streaming down her face. As she looked at the red rose on her lap that she had once been embarrassed about, she stood up and walked over to the closed casket where the physical body of her mother was now laid to rest. She gently placed the rose on the wooden tomb as she whispered, "I love you forever Momma."

As Sophia walked back to take her seat she noticed a small pink envelope laying on her seat. She picked it up and placed it gently on her lap and the only words on the envelope were Sophia Rose. As she neatly tucked the envelope into her dress pocket, Sophia felt a weight being lifted off her chest and it became easier to breathe once again. She was dazed for the remainder of the service and it felt to her as if she was so detached that she was watching a movie of the funeral before her very eyes. The cast of characters walking up to her one by one and offering her their condolences could have easily been actors on a big screen, and as the day progressed, Sophia took solace in her own numbness.

By the end of the day she sat quietly in her room, alone and feeling empty inside. The emotions she was experiencing were none that she had ever felt before, and she appreciated the moments of feeling nothing to the agony of feeling the pain of a broken heart. As her mind replayed the story that Pastor Abraham had told during the service, Sophia felt a very familiar energy around her. She knew this energy was her mom's and as soon as she felt that loving energy, the room was filled with the scent of a rose. "Momma?" Sophia cried out, but would not move in fear that the feeling and the scent would go away. If she was dreaming then she wanted to continue experiencing this dream. "Momma...I miss you so much. Please come back, please, I promise I will be good. I'll do anything you want me to do, just come back to me. I can't be here without you." As her tears turned to sobs, Sophia fell onto the bed and buried her face in her pillow. The pain in her heart was too heavy to bear and she cried out for relief of this agony and for her mom to make it better. The more she wished for her mom, the more Sophia realized that she would never be there to comfort her again, wipe away the tears, and tuck her into bed.

Sophia cried herself to sleep and when she awoke several hours later, she could still smell the faint scent of roses. Pulling herself up from her bed, Sophia remembered the pink envelope that she had found on her seat at the church and had earlier placed into her pocket. As she pulled the envelope out of the pocket of her wrinkled dress, Sophia recognized the writing as her mom's. It was in the same color envelope that her Daddy had given her days before, but the handwriting was definitely her mom's. As Sophia wiped her tear stained face, she sat back and began reading her letter.

My Dearest Sophia,

God is Real!

The most important lesson I can teach you is that God is real! You may not understand the power of these words at this moment, but you will. You see, God is sometimes difficult to find because he is so much a part of you that you often miss him in the moments you should be seeking him. I have had encounters with God and he is as real as you are. He speaks through your soul and His voice is heard as loudly as the conversations that you have with your father, but you must be open to communicating with Him and allowing him to speak to you as well. There is nothing frightening about His presence as he is the epitome of love and when you are in His presence, you feel so connected that you are one with him. His words are spoken through your thoughts but they are differentiated through the content of His message.

Learn to speak to Him daily and never again doubt that your prayers are not heard. For God hears every sound that you make, whether it is a prayer through your thoughts and tears when you are at a loss for words, or a prayer of gratitude when you are joyous for your blessings. The only way you will develop a relationship with Him is to acknowledge that he is so ever present within you because there is no separation. The more you develop your relationship with God, the more you will comprehend my words. Just as you work on maturing a relationship with your father or your friends, you must take the same amount of time and energy to cultivate a relationship with God. Take 30 minutes out of each and every day to be alone in silence through meditation or prayer and harvest your relationship with your maker. As you are co-creating your life with God and you must dedicate yourself to understanding it and appreciating it.

Your soul longs for connection and communion with God and when you choose not to honor your soul's calling then you are responsible for the severing of your most important connection to love and to self-love. Respect the power of love and know that your soul seeks to connect with your Source energy freely and you must honor your calling. Always put communion with the divine as your priority, whether you think you are too busy to or not. You choose how to create your time and if you spend 24 hours in a day by choice in not connecting with your life force, then you will suffer through sorrow and a feeling of disconnect to something greater than yourself.

Just as God is real, Jesus is just as real but he appears to me in the most brilliant colors I have ever seen! If I could explain what these colors appear to me like I would not do them justice because they are magnified hues and light combined to form the most amazing and beautiful appearance you could imagine. Sophia, if I could paint you a canvas you still would not appreciate the magnificence of his beauty! Jesus came first to me in colors and then again in human form and he is a beautiful and loving soul. Trust that through God and Jesus you have the relationship to heal from your broken heart. You must first allow yourself time to grieve and then grant yourself permission to heal and smile once again.

They will be your light that shines through you into that darkness that you have been swallowed into. They will both appear to you in dreams, together because they are one. You will know that these visits are more than just dreams because they will share with you messages of truth and words of hope. They will light your spirit and reignite the life back into your soul to make you want to truly live life to the fullest like you have never done before, Honor them, trust them, and love yourself enough to develop a magical relationship with them.

In the two different instances that I have connected with them in dreams, there was no judgment or condemnation. Their presence was love in its purest form and their messages were to bring comfort and hope. Release the fears that you have developed from listening to the voices of the world around you. For these are the same voices that walk alone in fear and relish in creating more fear in others.

If you walk blindly then you are responsible for your free will and accountable to only you for your choices. For with everything in life there is a cause and an effect and you can control more of your life than you have ever imagined just by controlling your thoughts, emotions, and actions. Most importantly, you create a life of love through connecting with and maintaining a relationship with love in its purest form which is God and Jesus Christ. They are not standing on a throne judging your every move, rather they are a part of your journey and wish to be present in your life through your every move. There is a huge difference because the first is based on love and the other in fear, and love and fear cannot be present simultaneously. Where love is, fear cannot reside.

Trust that your prayers are being heard and learn to count your blessings. Get into the habit each and every day when you awake to say a prayer of gratitude before your feet hit the floor and once again before you retire for bed every night. You will learn that the more you find in your life to be grateful for, the more blessings you will have in your life.

I love you forever,

Momma

The Power of Forgiveness
Chapter 8

Sophia was surprised how tired she became after the loss of her mom, as all she wanted to do was sleep. Nothing interested her anymore and she found herself distracted and her mind wandering during her class lectures. As Sophia's attention slipped, so did her grades and the once studious and creative young girl she once remembered herself to be was slowly transforming into someone that even she didn't recognize anymore. The stylish young girl that once laid awake at night mentally selecting her wardrobe for school the next day was completely disinterested in how she looked and what she loved about fashion now just became a burden of trying to find clothes that weren't black. She lost interest in writing and sewing and all Sophia wanted to do was sleep and sit alone in her quiet room.

The pain of watching her mom battle cancer was now overtaken by the despair of every part of her soul, and although people tried to warn her about the impending loss of her sick mom, nobody could have prepared Sophia for the amount of physical and emotional pain that a person suffers when they grieve. The light from the sun would hurt Sophia's eyes and sounds that she once enjoyed from music and laughter now hurt her ears and pierced through them like a knife. The heaviness of her chest bore the emotional burden of the longing she had for her mom and as each day passed, Sophia grew more and more depressed. No longer did she have the energy to carry on conversations let alone nourish her friendships with her group of friends, and just getting through the day became a victory.

As Sophia fell into depression her father realized that he was losing his little girl and could not deal with losing another person that he loved. Although he could not save his wife from cancer, he could help his daughter by getting her a professional who could assist her through understanding and processing her grief. Everyone in Sophia's life was noticing the change in her personality, appearance, and declining grades. Even though Sophia's teachers were being very understanding about her losing her mom, they were also growing more concerned about her lack of attention and sliding grades. They knew she was a bright child and felt helpless as they watched her each day growing into her own dark grief.

After a brief meeting with Sophia's teachers, her father decided to call a Grief Counselor that had been recommended to him by one of the teachers. He realized that time was of the essence if he wanted to help her, because as each day passed, so did the recognition of his little girl. The clothes that once fit her comfortably were hanging on her tiny body that was quickly losing weight. Although he tried to make her favorite foods, Sophia found it difficult to eat because of her loss of appetite and forcing herself to eat would only make her sick to her stomach.

When Sophia's dad sat her down one evening and tried to connect with her once again, just as he had done every night after her mom's death, he carefully brought up the idea of going to a grief counselor. Sophia looked at him with the same empty gaze that he had seen from her every day, the same gaze that replaced her once twinkling eyes. She listened as he explained how worried he was about her, and that he could not bear the thought of losing his only child now or ever. As he spoke, Sophia saw his hands tremble and his voice begin to crack from the emotions he was fighting to keep in. At that moment, Sophia realized for the first time that her dad was dealing with the same painful emotions that she had been experiencing, and for a brief moment a pang of guilt hit her hard. How could she be so selfish and not even think about her dad suffering through the emotional pain of losing his wife and soul mate?

Even though Sophia didn't like the idea of going to a grief counselor, she empathized with her dad and wanted to do something to bring him relief of some of his pain. She realized that by going to see a counselor, she would lessen the burden of his worry for her and allow him even an ounce of comfort that may ease his pain. As she agreed to see a grief counselor, Sophia's thoughts turned to concern that she had not even realized how her grief had turned to depression and how much she had changed. She slowly became more concerned and worried that she may not ever find her way out of this dark abyss. She doubted that a stranger could help her out of this darkness, but since her dad was so worried about her she agreed to see one the next day.

As Sophia waited in the lobby of the counselor's office with her dad, she looked around at the office walls filled with paintings of abstract art. Although she never saw herself as a talented artist, she giggled to herself that some of these pieces looked like something she could paint. One piece in particular was filled with splashes of vibrant colors that could have been thrown from a bucket of paint while the artist was standing over the canvas. As Sophia observed the artwork, her dad noticed a smile covering her once saddened face. "What are you smiling about honey" he asked out of curiosity because he had not seen her smile since the funeral just weeks ago. As Sophia explained to him her humor with the art work on the walls, he looked around and took notice of them. "Maybe the counselor couldn't cut it as an artist and decided to go to school to help people instead," he heard himself say and just then Sophia burst into laughter and they both laughed so hard that tears started streaming down both their faces. The harder they laughed, the more they cried, which in turn perpetuated more laughter.

As they both began to catch their breath and regain their composure, Sophia's dad stared at her for what seemed to be a very long time. "It's good to see you smile again Sophia," he whispered. "I've missed you." Sophia looked up at her dad to see tears welling in his eyes, except this time they were not tears of laughter but of sorrow. As she looked down at her lap, the feelings of guilt once again struck her like a lightning rod into her heart. "I'm sorry Daddy," she said. "I'm sorry that I never asked you how you are dealing with momma's death, and I'm sorry that I was ever mean and sassy to momma. As hard as she fought to hide them, the tears began streaming down her delicate face and she burst into tiny sobs. They embraced one another so tightly as if someone or something were pulling them apart. Sophia felt comfortable in her dad's arms but the realization that she would never feel the touch of her mom's arms around her began drawing her back into the all familiar feelings of despair.

Their attention quickly turned to the door that had just opened and an older woman with shoulder length gray hair was standing at the doorway. "Sophia, it is so nice to meet you...I'm Dr. Ann Archer." As the counselor walked towards them, Sophia noticed that she had a slight limp in her gait as if one leg were somehow slightly shorter than the other. Although her limp was noticeable Ann walked with the grace and poise of a ballerina, and her energy felt pleasant to be around. The Counselor explained to Sophia's dad that she would like to talk to her alone for this session and as they walked down the hallway together, Sophia's dad felt heaviness lift from his chest. Knowing this counselor came highly recommended, he had a deeper belief that she would somehow be able to help Sophia escape this trap of depression and sorrow that she had slowly sank into.

As Sophia walked into the room with Ann, she quickly took her seat and nervously clasped her hands in front of her and placed them on her lap. Avoiding all eye contact with Ann, Sophia began staring at the floor first then slowly moved her gaze around the room that was filled with framed diplomas. She couldn't help but be impressed with the accomplishments that Ann had earned throughout her career and suddenly Sophia felt a breath of hope flow through her body. If Dr. Archer could be this knowledgeable about the human behavior then maybe she could eventually help Sophia become happy again. It felt like years since she experienced happiness and the pain in her heart was growing burdensome. Sophia noticed the silence in the room and suddenly looked at Ms. Archer who was smiling at her and observing her.

As their eyes met, Sophia's fear slowly became replaced with calm and she became more comfortable sitting in the room. As Ms., Archer explained her background and purpose for helping others, Sophia silently listened and became more impressed by this woman who was speaking to her like an adult rather than a child. "Sophia, tell me a little bit about yourself," Dr. Archer finally said. As Sophia began to speak, she found it difficult to answer so she told Dr. Archer about her love for reading and her passion for ballet. The more Sophia spoke, the more interested Ms. Archer became, and she sat in silence for a few minutes while she listened to Sophia describe her favorite color and foods. When Sophia felt as if she said enough, she looked at Ms. Archer and stared at her for a few seconds before Dr. Archer finally spoke.

"Sophia, can you tell me about your mom?" Those words made Sophia uncomfortable and as she shifted nervously on her chair, her gaze went back to staring at the floor instead of Ms. Archer. "I can't," she replied as she heard her voice begin to strain under her breath. "Why not?" replied Ms. Archer, "because I'm afraid that if I talk about her then it will be as if she isn't here anymore." Suddenly Sophia's composure crumbled and she broke into tears which turned into deep sobs. Ms. Archer handed her a tissue from the box that was sitting on a small desk next to her and she thought to herself, *Poor baby, there's grief... and then there's this.* Dr. Archer took a deep breath and as she exhaled she closed her eyes and silently prayed, *God, please give me the proper words to help this little girl. She is in so much pain and needs your comfort now. I can't do this without you.*

Dr. Archer finally spoke again, "Sophia it is ok to talk about your mom. It allows you to share your feelings about her love and gives you permission to begin healing your heart." Sophia never looked up but continued crying into her tissues. After several moments of silence, Dr. Archer leaned over and gently placed her hand on Sophia's lap and finally spoke, "Sophia, what is the funniest memory you have of your mom?" Sophia looked up at Dr. Archer, and stared at her as if she was surprised by the question." After some deliberation Sophia looked back at Ms. Archer and proceeded to share several stories of shopping excursions that she experienced with her mom, and as Sophia spoke the stress that covered her expression began to disappear and her tears were slowly being replaced with smiles. Once she began conversing with Ms. Archer, Sophia began to relax more and cry less. Allowing her to finish her story, Ms. Archer then asked Sophia, "What one memory do you have of your mom that makes you smile?"

Sophia searched her memory for a moment and began to smile as she explained to Dr. Archer, "Momma and I used to write each other letters and leave them in hidden places that were hard to find. She would hide them in my thermos in my lunchbox, or sneak them into my shoes that I was wearing for school that day. I would hide hers in her jewelry box, put them under the cushions of her chairs, or somewhere in her purse. It was a nice surprise finding the letters because they were unexpected, but all of them made me feel special. They made me feel that whatever was happening throughout the day, I knew she loved me. One time I hid a letter in a really good spot and completely forgot that I hid it from her. I taped a letter and hid it underneath a big vase that had roses my dad had given her for her birthday. She didn't find the letter until she went to throw the roses away and wash the vase." As Ms. Archer listened, Sophia proceeded.

"There was one letter in particular that I wrote her and really wanted her to read it. I wrote the letter when momma got really sick and had to be in bed right before...." as Sophia' voice dropped, her eyes looked down at her lap. She paused for several moments then proceeded, "before she died." She whispered those words so low that they were nearly inaudible, but allowed herself to continue with her story. "You see, when dad told me that mom was going to die, I got really scared and then really angry. I didn't want to write her letters anymore because I was mad that she was going to leave me and I wanted to punish her. After I stopped writing her notes, I went into momma's room one day when she was sleeping. I sat next to her on the bed very quietly so I wouldn't wake her up. She didn't even know I was there and I felt really bad that I had gotten mad at momma for setting sick. I wrote her a letter and wanted to wake her up to give it to her but I felt so bad and so ashamed of myself that I just sat there next to her and watched her sleep. I tried to memorize what momma looked like when she was sleeping, and how her breath sounded, because I was afraid that I might forget her. "

Dr. Archer studied Sophia thoughtfully, and sensed relief from this young girl as she continued to share her story. "What was in the letter Sophia?" Dr. Archer asked, as she suddenly noticed Sophia's big brown eyes begin to well with tears. "In my letter to momma I asked for her forgiveness for being so mean to her when dad told me that she was going to die. You see, I told momma that if she loved me then she wouldn't leave me now. She should have gotten better and I got mad at her and went into my room and shut the door. I wrote in the letter that I didn't believe in God anymore and would never pray again because he didn't hear my prayers. I left momma there lying in bed hearing those words I told her over and over again in her head, and I was so ashamed of myself that I never apologized to her for saying those things.

The letter I wanted to give momma said how sorry I was that I said those things, and told her that I knew she loved me with all of her heart. I wrote her a poem that I wanted her to have so she wouldn't be afraid of dying alone. Even though I was so mad at God for making momma sick, I wanted her to know that I did believe he existed and that God would be there for her went she went to heaven." Sophia stopped for several seconds and despite her efforts to contain her tears, she wept. The pain in her face was so evident and Dr. Archer could not help but feel sorry for this beautiful girl who at such a young age was carrying the weight of the world on her tiny shoulders.

Dr. Archer sat silent, and lowered her gaze to her lap as she waited for Sophia to regain her composure. *Please God, please help me reach this little girl. Give me the words to ease her pain and allow your mercy to flow through her spirit so she can forgive herself and heal her heart.* As Dr. Archer finished her silent prayer she looked back up at Sophia. "Did you give your mom the letter?" she asked. Sophia shook her head, "no... I took the letter with me in case dad found it. I didn't want to get in trouble because I don't think he knew what had happened.

So instead of giving momma the letter, I went into the family room and threw it into the fireplace. Before I set it on fire, I asked God to forgive me and find a way to let me tell momma myself how sorry I was. As I watched the letter burn, I realized for the first that momma was going to die. She passed away before I had a chance to tell her how sorry I was." Tears streamed down Sophia's cheeks and her face revealed the pain that her heavy heart was experiencing.

"All I could think about was that momma had to die afraid that she may be alone and that there may not be a heaven. Every time I see a cross, or drive past a church, or even remember Pastor Abraham, I feel more and more ashamed that I never apologized. I'm afraid that God is mad at me and now I don't pray anymore. There are so many times that I want God to give me a sign that momma made it to heaven, but when I want to ask him for that sign then I think about how disappointed he must be in me and then I become more disappointed in myself. I don't pray, and I don't think I deserve to be loved anymore because I was so mean to momma." Dr. Archer watched Sophia as she caught sight of a beautiful red cardinal that perched itself on top of a tiny branch of the tree that stood outside of the window.

Sophia studied the bird as it moved closer to the window and pecked its beak against the glass. It stood on the tree limb and studied Sophia, then as quickly as it came, the cardinal quickly flew away. Sophia smiled as she remembered that cardinals were her mom's favorite bird. She loved the bright red color and she told Sophia that whenever you see a cardinal, then you will have good luck and fortune for that day. "Sophia,' Dr. Archer said in her pleasant voice. "What if you wrote your mom another letter, and this time since you cannot give it to her in the physical sense, after you write your words that you once wrote for her to read, then place the letter in a tiny pink envelope as you did with all of your previous letters to her, and do something ceremonial that will allow you to release those feelings of guilt that you are carrying inside of you." Sophia turned her attention back to Dr. Archer and shook her head, "it's too late, and momma won't get the letter because she already died."

Dr. Archer paused, and asked, "Do you believe that your mom went to heaven?" Sophia looked down at her lap and remained silent. "Sophia, do you remember what you wrote in that letter that you burned?" Sophia shook her head, and looked back to Dr. Archer and continued to listen. "I think if you write another letter to your mom and ask for her forgiveness, explaining to her that you were afraid when you got angry at her, then I think you might feel better. If there is even the slightest amount of faith that you believe God exists, then ask him for forgiveness in that letter. Allow yourself to write the words you once wrote to your mom, and although she did not receive the letter before she passed, if that tiny seed of faith will allow you permission to hope, then maybe she will read your letter from heaven. This may allow your heart to heal and may allow you to forgive yourself for this burden you have been carrying. Are you willing to do that?" Sophia nodded in agreement then said, "Dr. Archer I don't remember the poem I wrote momma. I had written a poem in that letter telling momma not to be afraid of dying, and I don't remember it now. She will never receive my poem and I am so ashamed that she was so scared when she died that God wouldn't be with her. I didn't mean to shake her faith, I was just so mad because my own faith had been shaken. It's too late to tell her not to be afraid of dying."

Dr. Archer convinced Sophia to write the letter anyway and although she could not remember the poem she had once written her sick mother, she could at least tell her in the letter that she hoped she was not afraid when she died. Sophia agreed to write the letter and perform the ceremony of burning it in the fireplace when she was done with it. As Dr. Archer spoke with Sophia's dad in private, Sophia sat in the waiting room pondering her session with Dr. Archer. She wasn't sure if this was a waste of her time or not because she was walking out of the office feeling as miserable as she did when she walked into it, but at least she met with the Dr. and hopefully allowed her dad to have a moment of peace. The sadness in her heart was so heavy, it felt as if a knife was cutting her chest open and the physical pain of this made Sophia feel as if she were drowning and there was no life raft in sight.

That evening after dinner, Sophia washed the dishes and began walking to her bedroom so she could be alone, just as she did every night after her mom had passed away. She heard her dad calling for her and walked into the living room where he was sitting comfortably on a chair with a book in his hand. "Sophia, Dr. Archer told me that you were supposed to do something for her tonight. Do you remember what that was?" Sophia remembered the letter that she had promised Dr. Archer she would write and burn tonight. "Yes," she responded. As he looked at Sophia with interest, she informed him that she would write it in her bedroom and complete the assignment Dr. Archer asked her to do.

As she sat on the bed, Sophia stared at the blank piece of paper in front of her and closed her eyes. She did not want to write this letter, but out of respect for her dad and for Dr. Archer, she proceeded to write. This time the words seemed harder to write and after realizing that she was not going to remember her old letter verbatim, she would write what was in her heart. She didn't have the heart to tell Dr. Archer that she felt this was an exercise in futility, but since her dad knew about the letter, she would write it anyway and perform the all-important burning ritual. As Sophia reached for the pen she stared at the paper once again and started recalling the moments of her day. The red cardinal that appeared at Dr. Archer's office window made her smile, especially since she believed that cardinals were a sign of good luck. The last thing Sophia remembers before falling asleep was feeling so fatigued that she could sleep for days.

When Sophia awoke, she was laying on top of her crumbled blank paper that Dr. Archer wanted her to write a letter on. She felt disappointed that she fell asleep before the letter could be written, but so happy that she was able to sleep the entire night. She could smell fresh coffee being brewed and as Sophia closed her eyes to fall asleep once again, the faint scent of roses filled her room. Barely awake, Sophia thought she was dreaming until the scent grew stronger. Sophia opened her eyes and pulled herself up as she looked around the room expecting to find roses sitting in a vase near her. Instead she realized that the scent of roses lingering in the air was not at all connected to the flowers. As she pulled herself from the bed to wash her face, Sophia noticed that she had fallen asleep in the same clothes that she had worn the day before. They were wrinkled and the sight of her appearance made Sophia's heart break once again.

She thought to herself that if her mom was still here, she would have woken her up and helped her change into her favorite pajamas before tucking her neatly into bed. Sophia realized that her mom would never be around to tuck her in, make her lunch, or help her pick out her clothes for her prom. The familiar pang of heartache hit Sophia once again and as she walked to the bathroom, Sophia's anger began to stir and as she walked past a vase filled with beautiful lily's that someone had given her earlier that week, Sophia grabbed the vase and hurled it across the room. As it crashed against the wall, Sophia stood in silence as tears streamed down her face. Both shocked and regretful, Sophia began picking up the pieces of broken glass that fell on the carpet. The only thing that kept the vase from shattering into tiny pieces was her lack of aim, and instead the vase broke into larger pieces that were easier to clean up. As she stood up to get a towel for the water that covered the carpet, Sophia carefully picked up a larger piece of glass and noticed a small pink envelope taped on the other side of it. She caught sight of the words on the piece of paper with the handwritten words, *Sophia Rose*.

Sophia felt her heart skip a beat as she recognized her mom's handwriting on the front of the envelope. Standing in shock as she stared at the envelope taped to the bottom of the broken vase, Sophia carefully picked up the broken glass and pulled the envelope from the tape. Her hands trembled as she sat on the corner of her bed and opened the envelope...

My Dearest Sophia,

The Power of Forgiveness

This lesson is a big one my little girl because as you read these words, you are in fact suffering at the hands of your own judgment. I have watched you struggle with forgiveness since the moment of my passing, and I have waited for the opportunity to explain this lesson to you in ways you will be open to hearing but most importantly, open to forgiving. These past few months have been so difficult for you because you hold on to the pain of not forgiving, and it is time you release this pain once and for all. The struggle you experienced when you first learned of my illness, to the pain and sorrow of not moving forward in the healing process, has taken its toll on you my beautiful daughter.

You must experience the root of your unforgiving rather than denying it, or you will not be able to release its hold on you. I know you are experiencing feelings of unforgiveness towards Daddy for not making me better, you have feelings of unforgiveness for my leaving you at such a young age, and you are most importantly experiencing the pain of not forgiving yourself for your anger towards me before I passed away. All of this pain is taking its toll on your spirit and depriving you of the energy to move forward, yet you are to "stuck" in the feeling of being miserable that you can't move forward into healing.

Let me explain that experiencing feelings of anger, fear, and guilt are all normal in this human experience, but you are not supposed to remain trapped in those fears. Where the root of your pain exists also lies the healing. You cannot continue running away from those feelings that make you experience fear or you will never heal them. Sophia you must allow yourself to experience the thoughts and the emotions at the root of the pain so you can sever the cord and set yourself free. You deserve this and so do I.

It is almost as if you have become connected to the feeling of loss and you believe this is the only memory of me that keeps me alive. In fact this could not be any further from the truth, as the feelings of fear keep you from connecting with me on a soul level because fear and love cannot co-exist. When you allow yourself permission to heal, then you know that you are in a genuine place of forgiveness and the healing power of love will set you free. You don't need to feel anger towards yourself in order to keep yourself connected to me. You have only to realize that you made the right choice at the time with the knowledge that you had – just like Daddy did when he didn't share with you how sick I really was.

You see, we both made the decision to keep the truth from you thinking that this decision was made in love, when in fact it was made in fear. I only wish that you understood how much we both wanted to protect you from the truth of my illness, and the pain you would have experienced dealing with the anticipation of my passing. I realize now that truth would have been the best option, because God would have prepared you on a soul level that I could not have understood. As parents, we try to do the best we can for our children and even though we may have the best of intentions – we are still human. Don't fault us for loving you and wanting to protect you, and in essence that is exactly what you have done to Daddy and me.

Except now you are harboring feelings of anger and because I am no longer in the physical world, you have turned them inward into anger towards yourself. Sophie you are feeling guilty for being angry at me, and these negative feelings are weighing you down so much that you can't heal from my passing. You must release those feelings and allow yourself the freedom to move forward.

The only way that you can you can heal your pain is to go to the root of it and sever the cord that attaches your heart to that pain. If you fail to heal your soul, then the pain that is stronger than your feelings of self-love will overpower you. When this happens then subconsciously you create life experiences to support that internal pain. This is why you often witness beautiful and intelligent young women with boyfriends or friends who belittle them and disempower them. It is because inside, they are already feeling those emotions and they choose people to surround them who will support it.

Until these people realize that they must first validate and heal themselves, then they will continue making the same choices. Validation first comes from within and when you choose on a deliberate level to become happy, then you will make conscious choices that support your goal of feeling happy. You will rarely experience having people in your life who make you feel good if you feel miserable on the inside. Oftentimes you will support those feelings of misery by choosing people to surround you who support those feelings.

In order to change your feelings of fear into feelings of love then you must focus on those feelings and release the pain. The best way to heal the pain is to get to the core of that pain and see it for what it is....something that you can change with your perception of what you focus on. You have the right to heal your heart and soul without worry that the experience that created those feelings will define you...it won't. You are not defined by the pain of my loss any more than I am defined by the illness that took me from you.

Forgiveness is a choice that lies within your own control even though you experienced a situation that you felt you had no control over. Forgiveness is a tool provided to you by God to allow one soul to take control of a situation that they experienced from fear, and release that experience into the love and light of the Holy Spirit. You have held onto fear of losing me to cancer which you had no physical control over, and how deeply that has affected you into believing the illusion that you no longer have control over anything. This false belief now has placed you in a deeper state of fear and it is beginning to take control over you.

The only truth we have in this experience through life is that we can only control our thoughts, emotions, and actions. In fact the only person and situation you ever need to have control over in order to experience love and joy is yourself. Once you choose to release the actions of another person which have created fear in your own life, you grant yourself permission to not only heal in love, but take complete control over your own life in any situation that comes into your experience whether you feel in control over it or not.

Forgiveness is one of the most powerful tools you have in your life my child, because it allows you to re-experience the situation that brought you negative emotions and take control over it on a grander scale. While I was in physical form fighting this disease, you realized that you could not control anything in this experience and the fear almost crippled you. Now that you understand the power of forgiveness to heal yourself, you will take these words and you will soon control this situation in a way you never thought possible.

Your words will reach many souls who need to heal their own life through imprints left by another person or situation that caused them pain. As someone who loves to write my child, you will take that passion and use it to control your own healing by providing it to another. I have read your life chart and am so proud of you because you are slowly moving beyond the pain of an uncontrollable situation and are moving into a place of love and healing for your growth. This does not disconnect you from me, instead it moves you closer to me in spirit because your heart is releasing the fear and replacing it with love.

Meanwhile, in order to continue the healing process you must be deliberate in your thoughts, emotions, and actions. Discover ways to release the pain through performing those actions that you love to do. Since your passion lies in writing, then write out your feelings and release them so your heart no longer has to hold them so tightly. You enjoy running, so run every day and allow the crisp air to reignite your numb senses so you can feel alive through every cell in your body again.

If you must stand in front of the mirror every day and look yourself in the eye and say, "I forgive myself and love myself enough to release fear and embrace love. I deserve to be free from guilt." Repeat this pattern daily until you no longer find it difficult to look yourself in the eyes and acknowledge yourself. Guilt and pain are not the root of what bonds us, as love and a soul connection will keep us united forever. You lost me once my darling daughter, so stop trying to relive the pain of my loss every day. By moving forward you can continue on your journey into the rest of your live, but your life is in this moment. Forgive yourself my love, and remember that I will always be just a thought away.

I love you forever,

Momma

As Sophia stared at the letter, she noticed that the scent of roses had dissipated and the only scent that lingered in the air was the smell of coffee. The beautiful letter she held in her hands brought a feeling of such tender love that for a moment Sophia knew what it felt like to be happy again. Sophia tried to push aside the questions and confusion that were crossing her mind, as she embraced the feeling of love and warmth that her heart was feeling right now. The tenderness she was experiencing brought such needed comfort that Sophia closed her eyes and relished in the warmth of the loving glow.

As Sophia turned the final page, she noticed a small red stain at the top of the page and as she read the title of the page, Sophia felt the blood draining from her face and her entire body grew ice cold. *I don't understand,* she thought to herself. *How can this be possible?* As Sophia read the words, *My Father* at the top of the page, she realized that the page she held in her hand was in fact the poem she had written for her mom just months ago. As she stared at the tattered corners of the pages, she discovered the stain of the cranberry juice she had spilled on the corner just after writing it.

There was no doubt that this was the same poem that she had regretted not giving her mom, but instead chose to burn along with the apology letter she threw into the fire. Sophia remembers being afraid that someone would find the letter and poem she had written for her mom, because she was so ashamed that she didn't want anyone to read the words. She knew the fire had consumed these pages because she watched them burn into ashes with her own eyes. How then was she holding the poem in her hand?

My Father

I'm yet but a child now my Father I have so much to learn;
Will you guide me and teach me, for your presence I yearn.
I began school today my Father there is so much to see;
Will you be at my side, I'm frightened...stay here with me.

I'm growing slightly gawky now Father I wish I could hide;
Stay with me Father, right here by my side.
I'm maturing now Father, I'm 18 and oh so grown!
My dreams will soon lead me to a path yet unknown.

Hold my hand Father I'm not old enough yet;
I still need your guidance, forever my love and respect you will
get.
I'm marrying today Father, I'm so certain – so sure;
You have certainly blessed me, he's shared with me your love
– so abundant and pure.

I'm frightened now Father this child is not yet born;
How will she survive a world full of bitterness and scorn?
I'm so busy today Father so much yet to do!
Can you please wait a moment; I don't have much time now
for you.

I'm watching my child now Father, I'm so grateful you've
raised her;
Can you see the love in her eyes; she's your child for sure.
I'm so tired now my Father, in this weary body I must rest;
My life has been so fulfilling, I pray I've passed life's great test.

I've loved and I've lost – I've surrendered more times than I've won;
Yet the one remaining certainty has been Jesus your son.
I'm ready now Father, take me in the peace of the night.
Your Angels have come down to meet me, comfort me from my fright.

I have only one prayer now Father, one final request.
That you guide my dear daughter, even as an adult at her best.
Let her never feel lonely, and hear her faintest of moan;
For wherever she is my Father, with you she's never alone.

I'm sorry Momma and I love you forever,

Sophia Rose

Turn Your Pain into Power
Chapter 9

The remainder of the week was a mental blur to Sophia, and she found herself in a continued state of feeling numb. As if she were watching herself perform throughout the day in class and have conversations, but she couldn't remember actually feeling anything but pain in her heart. Sophia felt less and less interested in spending time with her friends, and wanted more and more to spend time alone in her room. She always felt tired and lacked energy, so she preferred to sleep rather than enjoying the activities that she used to love doing. She dropped out of cheerleading because she didn't have the energy or the enthusiasm to be a part of the team, and because she had been such good friends with most of her squad, they felt a sense of loss from her withdrawal.

Sophia found herself wondering about the letters she was receiving and how the poem she herself burned could have possibly been a part of the letter. As confusing as the letters were, they also served as a source of comfort for Sophia. As strange as these letters were to receive, Sophia knew that she needed a miracle to feel like her old self again and as much as she wanted that, Sophia knew that she would never be the same again...nothing would ever be the same again. Talking to Dr. Archer didn't help her much, but she felt comforted by the fact that there were people who wanted to help her.

As she waited for her session in Dr. Archer's office, Sophia looked once again at the paintings that surrounded the office walls. She smiled at the burst of laughter that she and her dad shared when they sat in this room just one week ago, and this time Sophia observed the paintings and they didn't seem so funny anymore. Now these pieces seemed to blend in with her spirit through the vibrant colors and energy they seemed to emote, and as her eyes wandered from painting to painting, she caught sight of one piece of art that caught her interest.

Dr. Archer observed Sophia as she looked around the room and after several moments of silence, Dr. Archer broke the silence. "Sophia, how are you feeling today?" she asked. "Fine," was all Sophia could manage to say. Dr. Archer watched as Sophia stared intently at one of the pieces of art hanging on her wall. "What do you think of that painting Sophia?" Dr. Archer asked. "I don't know," she replied but she never took her eyes off the painting. Do you like it?" she continued to question Sophia and finally she looked at Dr. Archer and said, "I think so...it's kind of pretty," Sophia replied, "What is it supposed to be?" Dr. Archer looked at the painting and asked Sophia what she thought it was. As Sophia studied the painting again, she took a long moment of silence and finally answered, "I don't know, but I thought that it was painted by a five year old when I first saw it."

As Sophia heard those words coming out of her mouth, she winced and wondered at what point during her grieving process she lost the filter from her head to her mouth. She looked apologetically at Dr. Archer who was smiling and chuckled under her breath. "It was actually painted by a client of mine," she responded. Sophia looked surprised and then looked back at the painting hanging on the wall. "Really?" Sophia asked, as she watched Dr. Archer walk towards the painting and remove it from the wall. "This painting looks as if it is just a canvas with paint thrown and swirled around it, but there is more to this than meets the eye."

Sophia sat upright and listened as Dr. Archer proceeded to share the story behind the art. "This painting was created by a beautiful young girl who claims that she saw God in her dream.

Actually it was Jesus she saw and as she tried to describe what he appeared like, she became more frustrated. You see this little girl was dealing with some very adult issues and she had lost a family member and like you, was dealing with some powerful feelings of depression. Since she was already so creative, I asked her to paint the vision of Jesus that appeared to her in a dream rather than attempt to describe him. She came back to see me several weeks later and brought this beautiful painting."

As Sophia listened intently to Dr. Archer, she turned her attention back to the painting and still didn't' understand how this could possibly resemble Jesus. Dr. Archer continued, "This young girl said that one night in a dream, Jesus came to her and told her that her mom was going home soon. As Jesus spoke to her, he appeared in colors so vivid that she described them as the most beautiful and vibrant colors she had ever seen. The reds were so vibrant and vivid, and the yellows danced in their bright, illuminated hues. She explained that she had never seen colors so bright and beautiful and as she witnessed the colors dancing in movement, she also felt such a powerful emotion of love that she had never experienced before."

Sophia's gaze remained fixed on the painting as she studied it for several moments. Dr. Archer searched her expression which seemed to soften the more she appreciated the painting that now had a new story of hope. "Sophia," Dr. Archer continued, "sometimes our greatest inspiration comes during the lowest moments of our life. This painting to some may appear as a work of elementary art, but behind the colors lies a story of spirituality, hope, and healing. What seems to be a canvas covered with abstract art to some is in truth a significant meaning to one young girl that there is life after death and Jesus can take many forms to many people. To some his vision has appeared as a bearded man in white clothing, and to others he appears as magical colors and benevolent energy. We each get to define our relationship with him and he gets to define his face to us. The ultimate goal is that we allow ourselves to remain connected to hope through our own definition of it."

Something in Sophia's heart felt lighter as if a heavy rock or burden had suddenly been lifted. Although she never shared with Dr. Archer the letters she had found, she took this message as allowing hope to enter her life and being in an attitude of gratitude for the magical letters she was receiving. Sophia was too emotionally and physically exhausted to try to make sense of them but she appreciated the fact that something magical was happening and if that magic was in allowing her brief moments of solace from her grief, then who was she to question it.

As Sophia lifted herself up from her chair at the end of her session, Dr. Archer surprised Sophia by offering the painting to her. "I don't normally offer my artwork to my clients," Dr. Archer explained, "but I saw how much this painting intrigued you, and I think you appreciate it for the message and for the art" said Dr. Archer. "Would you like to take it home?" Sophia was shocked as she smiled and nodded. The only thing Dr. Archer asked of Sophia was when she no longer felt a connection to the painting, if she could send it back to her. As Sophia walked down the hallway with the painting tucked underneath her arm, she felt a sense of pride that she got to take the painting home with her. She felt as if she won a valuable prize, and as she observed the paintings that she had once made fun of, she felt a sense of humility and appreciation instead.

Sophia's spirit was feeling better than it had in days as she explained to her dad about the visit to Dr. Archer and receiving this gift. She explained that she didn't understand the meaning behind the paintings that she saw in her office, and thought they were not created from talent because they didn't fit the mold of what she expected talent to be. She was also humbled by the fact that she learned not to judge something that appeared to be different because it is still beautiful to someone. As Sophia's dad listened intently, he smiled and recognized a sense of joy in her that had been dimmed since her mother's death. "What lesson did you learn today Sophia?" he asked. As she stared into the glass of milk on the table, Sophia pondered the lesson of the beautiful painting.

"I learned that to one person something may not appear beautiful, but when you go beneath the surface you discover that thing is more beautiful than anything you may ever see again," she replied. "I also learned not to judge a book by its cover, because there is something magical in every work of art." He leaned into Sophia and asked her, "Do you consider people works of art?" Sophia looked up at him and studied his face. "I do now. I learned in Dr. Archer's office today that what I thought was just a silly painting had meaning behind it. Daddy, this girl said she saw Jesus in her dream and the colors that she used to describe him were not vivid enough, or bright enough to even touch the magnitude of his beauty. She said that each color glowed within its own aura, and as the colors became more illuminated they grew iridescent and vibrant."

Sophia paused for a moment and closed her eyes, "I only wish that I could see Jesus. I want to ask him why he took momma when I prayed every night for God to heal her." Sophia's voice cracked under the strain but she didn't cry. "Daddy, do you think momma went to heaven?" Sophia's dad looked away briefly and examined the piece of art that Sophia sat on the counter when she brought it home from Dr. Archer. "Sophia," he answered slowly and deliberately, "I know that we learn our entire lives to have faith in God. Faith that will move mountains and part oceans, but oftentimes when something tragic occurs in a person's life they are called upon to stand in that unwavering faith. I believe that your mom is sitting next to God and watching you each and every day. I also believe that she is dancing as fast as she can in a body that is no longer sick and weary." He paused and let Sophia process what he was saying then continued, "I also believe that as humans we have the right to find our way to a greater faith through the sorrows and tragedies that we endure throughout our lives. "

As Sophia gazed back at the picture, she realized that she was so afraid that her faith had faltered and she wasn't sure anymore what she believed. "There are times Daddy," she said. "There are times that my heart hurts so bad that I can't even breathe, and I don't know if I'm ever going to feel good again. Today I stood by the window and watched a bird fly back and forth from a tree branch to my window sill, and I thought how lucky that bird must be to feel happy enough to chirp and sing. Daddy, sometimes my heart hurts so much and I get so tired that I don't know if I can make it anymore." She paused as she noticed the look of sadness and worry in her dad's eyes. "My body is so tired that it feels," Sophia paused and looked down at her lap. "What Sophie?" her dad asked. "What does your body feel?" Sophia looked up at him with tears welling in her big brown eyes. "My body feels like it doesn't have the strength to continue feeling this bad and I feel like my body is slowly shutting down."

Sophia's dad grabbed her and pulled her towards him as he held her tightly in his arms. He wanted so badly to take away the pain she was experiencing, but he felt helpless and defeated. *Please God,* he prayed silently. *Please ease her pain and bring Sophia comfort. I need you more than ever before, and I'm sorry that I too have lost faith in you. But if you bring comfort and peace to Sophia, I promise that I will pray again. This time I will expect your answer and listen rather than walk away.* As Sophia's dad released his embrace from her, he gently lifted her chin so her eyes would meet his. "Sophia, I too have been questioning my faith. I think we need to remind one another that God allowed your mom to have time with us so she could say good-bye. I know it was painful to watch her body deteriorate but maybe we can change our perspective and be thankful that although she suffered, we had time with her and got a chance to cherish our relationship with her in ways that many who are healthy and take life for granted don't get to appreciate."

This made sense to Sophia because although she was so frightened during her mother's illness, she was still grateful to grow closer to her than ever before. "Sophia," he continued, "I think that it is important to allow yourself time to grieve and miss your mom. I also believe in my heart that you can give yourself permission to heal when your heart and soul grow into that place in time. Don't feel that your connection to the pain will keep your connection to your mom, because oftentimes we begin to find the miracles appear in our lives as we heal. In other words, don't rush your healing process but allow yourself moments to laugh when your heart finds something funny, as well as moments to let her memory live on through you."

Finding time for healing was one thing Sophia wanted so badly in her life, but she also realized that there were moments that she wanted to laugh but wouldn't allow herself to because she felt ashamed that she was feeling happy about something. Sophia had not realized until now that she would not allow those moments in her day when she wanted to laugh or smile, or even play because she felt as if she were betraying her mom. After all, if her momma was not here and she began feeling the tiniest ounce of joy, then she feared that she may forget her as the days progressed and nothing frightened Sophia more than forgetting her mom.

"Daddy, I'm afraid that I will forget momma. What if I begin laughing and making jokes again and I forget what momma looked like, or the things she loved, or even how she felt just being around momma. I'm so afraid that as my pain disappears so will my memory of her and I don't want that to happen...ever." As Sophia heard her own words escape her mouth she felt a sense of guilt being removed from her heart and began to breathe easier as if one more weight was lifted from her chest. "Sophia, you can never forget your mom," replied her dad. "You and mom have a connection that began so long ago before you were even born, because she knew you would come to her. She knew it like she knew that she was going to make spaghetti and meatballs for dinner. It was that obvious to your mom that she felt she was going to have a daughter and whenever she would talk about you before you were even born, a smile would cross her lips."

Sophia sat back on her chair and smiled as her dad recalled the months before she was even born, and how they planned for her and knew she would be named Sophia. Because her mom thought Sophia Lauren was the most beautiful woman and she loved roses because they signified love, joy, and blessings, the name Sophia Rose was created. "She loved you before she even conceived you," Sophia's father said gently with a voice that expressed such tenderness and love. "Sophia, you are connected to your mom and nothing can separate the love of a mother and her child, not in life and not even in death." He stopped talking for a moment and saw something in Sophia's face that he had not seen in months. He saw an expression of peace, and the more he studied his daughters face the more he realized that she resembled her mother.

"Your mom knew the moment you were conceived before anyone else did because she said that she felt you in her heart. She knew when your spirit entered her body and she cherished and nourished that connection with you long before you were ever born. Sophia, your mom didn't have to see you to know that you were alive and living inside of her body and her heart. She spent nights describing what you would look like when you were born and what personality you would have as you grew... something that she could not have known because she never laid eyes on you until your birth. If you had that connection with your mom without her even seeing you, then don't you think that you still have that same connection without seeing her now?"

A puzzled Sophia dropped her jaw open and looked completely dismayed. She had not even stopped to consider this, but as she took the time to contemplate this message, Sophia chimed in. "Is this where faith comes in Daddy?" she asked. "If I have faith in a God and Lord that I have never seen, then I need to have the same faith that momma is just as alive as they are but I just can't see her." The mere concept of this idea brought a bigger smile to Sophia's face and suddenly she felt the "life jacket" being thrown from the universe through this message. "I think I can get through some of the pain by remembering this, because it helps to understand it the way you described it Daddy."

As Sophia was being tucked into bed she felt the burden of the world had lifted from her heart and the act of breathing became easier that she had remembered it. Her dad placed a gentle kiss on her forehead and she looked up at him and smiled. "Thank you Daddy for sharing this with me. I love the story about how momma loved me so much, and I hope that I can someday remember her love again without getting sad." Sophia then turned to look at the painting that they hung in her room and said, "Do you think I will get to see Jesus some day?" Her dad looked at her and said, "I think you can see him in many ways as long as you remain open to however he chooses to appear to you. Until now, you may not have believed that Jesus can come to us in forms of energy, but we are all energy and connected to one another through that same energy. Yes Sophia, I think if you ask God for a miracle you will eventually see one in His time."

As her dad turned off the light and closed her bedroom door, Sophia asked in prayer for a miracle. *I won't tell you how my miracle has to come into my life; I will just keep my eyes open for it and accept it in the form it comes. Good night Father, please kiss my momma for me and tell her that I love her.* Sophia closed her eyes and for the first time did not cry herself to sleep, but instead relished in the comfort of the peace that filled her soul.

As Sophia rolled over in bed to catch sight of the beautiful art that hung on her wall, she wondered how loved the young girl must have felt when she dreamt of Jesus. The moonlight was so bright that the glow illuminated her room and made the painting that much more beautiful. As she stared at the painting, Sophia's eyes grew heavier and slowly closing them she caught a glimpse of something on the corner of her painting. She noticed a small piece of paper on the bottom right corner of her painting that appeared to be the artist's signature! Sophia bolted out of bed and turned on her lamp to study the name and as her eyes focused on the writing in the corner, tears began to fill her eyes. Moving closer to the painting she read the words of the artist signature, *Gracie Angelica Bello 1983*

Sophia stared at the signature and pulled the painting from the wall where it hung just seconds before. She sat on the corner of her bed and stared at the signature and year and her heart was beating so loudly that she could only hear the rhythm of the fierce pounding against her chest. How could this be? She thought as she thought back on the story that Dr. Archer had shared with her about the young girl who painted this work of art after having a dream of Jesus. "Momma," she whispered as she stared even closer at the painting. As Sophia pulled the framed canvas closer to her, and help it as she rocked back and forth on her bed. She looked at the painting and realized that the client Dr. Archer was referring to was in fact her mom when she was a young girl. As Sophia clutched the painting, she felt something on the back of the canvas and as she turned the painting over, she discovered a small envelope taped to the back of the painting. The tape was discolored due to the age of the painting, but the pink envelope was tucked underneath a piece of plastic that protected it from the elements.

Sophia carefully pulled the tape back and removed the envelope from the protective plastic, and as she turned it over she read the words, *Sophia Rose* in her mother's handwriting. Sophia burst into tears and this time she was crying from the mixed emotions of joy and confusion. As Sophia opened the envelope and removed the paper inside, a strong scent of roses filled the air. She looked around the room once again to see if there were any flowers in her room, but found none. Sophia leaned back and closed her eyes for a brief moment to pray that this was in fact real and that she was not dreaming. As Sophia opened her eyes, she read the letter that was written for her over what appeared to be 30 years ago.

My Dearest Sophia,

Turn Your Pain into Power

I have watched you crying tears of grief for so long, and your pain has literally overtaken your life. Slowly as you have been adjusting to the pain of a broken heart from my loss, your survival instincts have been adjusting to feeling depressed so you can adapt and move forward with your life. The problem is that as you have grown comfortable being uncomfortable in the pain of losing me, your mind, body, and soul have grown accustomed to pain being your new normal. This isn't good for you. In the process of adapting to your new "normal" you adopted the feeling of powerlessness and feeling out of control.

My dearest Sophia, I cannot stress to you enough the importance of turning your pain into power rather than burying it. When you try to conceal your hurt and ignore the pain, your heart still feels the sorrow, but your mind is in conflict trying to protect you and it becomes torn. Although your heart feels sorrow, your mind disconnects, then your soul is left to heal itself in the only way it knows how...through denial. By pretending that your heart is not hurting or your mind cannot focus on anything because it is still trying to deal with the pain of your loss, you do not allow yourself the chance to grow past this experience.

Turn your pain into power and instead of running away from it, embrace it and allow it to fuel your passion. The pain in your heart will drive you to seek yourself in the tiniest corners of your mind and provide you the desire to look within to discover yourself. What often happens though is that so many souls bury their pain, and once they disconnect from their source of truth, they have become disconnected from themselves. Once you separate from truth, then you have only illusion to deal with, and you end up creating your world in the limitations of illusions.

My dearest Sophia, please understand that you have the right to grieve, but in time allow yourself the courage to heal. It takes courage to know when to trust your soul and move forward from the pain you have been suffering. Remember this on any level, because pain and suffering of the soul cannot be diagnosed through x-ray machines or healed through Band-Aids and stiches. You must become aware and remain aware of how you are feeling at any moment in your life. Living in awareness creates intentions that will benefit you to greater fulfillment on your soul's journey.

There have been so many nights when I watched you cry yourself to sleep because the overwhelming sadness you carry in your heart is too much to bear. I have also witnessed you judge yourself for feeling so vulnerable and broken, that you begin lashing out at those you love because you are still dealing with the same pain...just different reactions throughout the day. As your soul heals, find a way to turn your pain into power by harnessing that pain and creating something beautiful from it. Do something you love and use the power of love in action to write a poem, or plant a beautiful tree in my memory, or even channel your energy into becoming a greater version of yourself through competing in a pageant. All of these are just examples of things that are action based that will allow you to transfer the energy of pain into purpose. You learned to walk one step at a time, and in the same manner your soul will heal by learning how to move forward one step at a time. In essence Sophia, you are learning how to walk again from the inside out, through healing from your pain in a very deliberate manner.

Don't lose yourself in your grief, for so many souls walk this journey through their life completely ignoring their own spirit. The pain you feel lies within your heart and soul, but that is also where you will find your healing. You cannot run from your own spirit because in your spirit resides the spirit of God, and the only way to heal is to connect yourself with the energy of the Divine Source. Never doubt if your prayers are being heard my love, for your prayers are felt through your energy and heard through your thoughts. There is not one prayer that goes unanswered, but remaining in the light of truth will allow you to recognize the voice of God from the chaos of the noises around you.

Believe in the power of your dreams again and once in a while, ask your father how he is doing. He worries so much about you that he has lost track of himself in the process of taking care of you. He isn't used to serving in the role of both parents, and I am worried for him. Your father has taken the burden of your grief and owned it as his own so he can help you first and himself last. As a result of this, your father has buried his sorrow which has the potential to turn into more pain if not dealt with completely. This would be a good lesson for him to learn this week Sophia, because he too has to learn to turn his pain into power...in a positive way. If only he would listen to my words when he dreams, but he has separated himself from me through his grief and he cannot understand this process.

You are a young girl who is more open to receiving my energy and believing in the power of life after death, so your openness allows you to receive my energy in this form. Just as God hears your prayers through thoughts Sophia, you are receiving my energy as well. You oftentimes hear my voice and look around for me, when in fact you heard my voice echoing in your mind. I am pure energy now beautiful child, and cannot be seen in the physical world as you saw me before. I can however, be heard and felt because my energy remains the same and you recognize me through my energy. This is why you have been open to me and allowing our connection to continue healing you through your pain.

There will come a day when you are grown and you won't need to hear my words as often or seek me and my energy as much because you are healing slowly. This does not mean that you love me less Sophia, it only means that you are allowing yourself time to heal and grow back into your own soul. You worry that letting go of the pain of losing me equates to letting go of me, but it is in fact the opposite. I represent love in your life rather than pain, so allow me to enjoy my role now on the other side. Love yourself more, laugh harder, and above all celebrate your life!

I will love your forever my precious child. I am so proud of you and always know that I am just a thought away.

I love you forever,

Momma

Mending Your Broken Spirit
Chapter 10

The next morning Sophia convinced her dad that she needed to see Dr. Archer again because she wanted to process more of her grieving. She chose not to tell him about the letter that she found behind the painting because a part of her thought that he was leaving them and another part of her thought that if he wasn't then there would be too many questions she could not answer. She also felt in her heart that this was very special, and didn't want anybody to take away the magic she was feeling by doubting her or ruining the special feeling she was experiencing.

As she walked into Dr. Archer's office with her dad by her side, she noticed the paintings on the walls had been removed and replaced with photos of oceans and lighthouses instead. Puzzled, Sophia and her dad checked in and were informed that Dr. Archer was no longer with their group and had to leave unexpectedly, so she packed her things and left. They were also informed that all of Dr. Archer's clients were referred to qualified colleagues who were capable of continuing to meet with Sophia and assist her through the grieving process. Shocked, Sophia asked if she could have Dr. Archers contact information but the receptionist informed her they were not allowed to disclose it.

"I can't believe this," Sophia mumbled under her breath as she looked at her dad in dismay. Sophia felt hurt and betrayed, but most importantly she wanted to ask Dr. Archer more about the painting, and now she would have to leave with so many unanswered questions. Sophia thought for a moment and wanted to peek in Dr. Archer's office to see if she could find anything else about her deceased mom. "Can I use the restroom please?" asked Sophia as she was directed from the receptionist that it was down the hall next to Dr. Archer's old office. As Sophia excused herself she moved cautiously down the empty hall and just before she walked to the bathroom door, Sophia noticed that Dr. Archer's office was empty except for a desk and a few pieces of paper next to a stack of pens.

Sophia slid into the empty office and without moving searched the room for anything that would answer her questions about the artwork that she was given; the same artwork that apparently was painted by her mother when she was a young girl. Feeling a sinking feeling in the pit of her stomach, Sophia began snooping through the desk drawers for anything that might tell her how to contact Dr. Archer. As she pulled open a small drawer on the side of the desk, Sophia noticed a large white envelope with the name *Sophia* written on it. She quickly grabbed the envelope and shoved it into her backpack and walked out of the office and briskly back to the reception area.

When Sophia got home, she told her dad that she had homework to do and ran up to her room and closed the door. As she pulled out the envelope that she found in Dr. Archer's desk drawer, she sat on the bed and opened it to find a pink envelope, this time thicker with what appeared to be more papers in it. A smile crossed Sophia's full lips as she pulled the paper from the envelope and began to read...

My Dearest Sophia,

Mending Your Broken Spirit

Life is an amazing journey that is filled with blessings and challenges, and as you have discovered...grief is one of the most difficult challenges you will ever face. Grief represents the loss of love, companionship, and connection from one so close to you that the experience of disconnect feels as if a part of you has died along with them. The feelings of loss and longing pull on your heart so hard that your body is trying to hold on to keeping itself together long enough so you can lay down and rest long enough to begin the process all over again in the morning. Sophia, I have watched you grieve and have witnessed the struggle your body is encountering through experiencing my loss.

Sounds have become more acute and your ears are so sensitive to all sounds around you. Even the slightest whispers are like drums pounding against your ears. Sight has become more vivid and the light that would normally bring pleasure to your eyes is now blinding you. Touch is beyond sensation because some part of your spirit has become so raw that you feel exposed to the elements of the world around you. If only you could somehow lessen the pain that your grief has created within you. If only you could lessen the pain that sustains you and keeps you in the realm of fear and survival. This pain will threaten to destroy you and this pain will also serve you as a catalyst to ultimately survive.

Sophia, only by deliberate thought will you create happiness amidst the struggle of sorrow you are encountering. Let us create your journal today to help you overcome your feelings of sadness and assist you in the healing process. It can become so easy to drown in your own grief and fear, so through deliberate creation you can overcome anything that your mind sets out to experience. Let us call this process "Mastering Your Greatness," because in the midst of fear lies a greater version of yourself. Through focusing your thoughts, emotions, and actions on becoming a greater version of yourself, then you are deliberately controlling some part of your life when it feels as if sorrow is beginning to control you.

Step by step and day by day you will write in your Mastery Journal and I will help you overcome the grief you are experiencing from my loss. Step by step I will show you how you can apply these tools to overcoming sorrow in any area of your life, and you will never become a victim to your own thoughts and emotions again. You will learn how to be a deliberate co-creator and stay focused on creating your life the way you want to experience.

Steps to Mastering Your Greater Self

Create what you want, not what you need

What do I mean when I instruct you to create what you want and not what you need? So many times throughout our lives, we settle for what we believe we should have instead of reaching for what we are worth. There is a significant difference because the Universe will mirror back to you exactly what you have created. If you desire to lose a certain amount of weight in time for your upcoming pageant, and you find that your goal is being compromised by your inability to stay out of the junk food drawer in the evenings, then you are in essence creating more weight for your body, if your desire to experience the goodies is greater than your desire to lose weight and get in shape. If your fear of not self-soothing is greater than your love for wanting to compete in top swimsuit shape, then the strongest emotion will always win.

In this specific example of compromising your fitness goals for junk food, you are getting what you need, not what you want. Your want is the desire to master your fitness goals, but your need is to have the instant gratification of comfort food. After you succumb to your own temptation, you revert back to getting angry with yourself for not being more disciplined. You create a theme in your life where your needs outweigh your wants and the cycle that follows creates feelings of being out of control, when in fact you are in control of the entire process.

When your mind thinks it is being denied something, it tends to crave that very thing even more. So rather than just deny your mind or body a certain habit, you must replace the habit with something else. Instead of reaching for the junk drawer for sweets, then go to the refrigerator for a fruit or healthy snack that is healthy and still satisfies your hunger craving. It is in the mind where your value is perceived, so you must tell yourself that the new food is better tasting, and better for your body. You create the value through your perception of it. If you reach for the fruit and think to yourself that this is a sad replacement for your junk food, then you will never change the habit.

You must redefine your goals through your specific ways of perception so your emotions and actions will follow. Think about what food or habits create for our lives. They become patterns of repetition and repetition creates a sense of comfort for us whether the habit is beneficial for us or not. Rather than trying to change the habit without changing your perceived value of it, you must alter the way you look at the habit you are trying to break. Stop for a moment and be connected to your senses so you can control what happens next. The only way you can be a deliberate creator is to be present in the moment of creation.

Connect yourself to the experience of what you want to create

The most memorable experiences I can recall from my life are the moments that I was most connected to through mind, body, and soul. When Daddy and I were trying to conceive you, I prayed so hard for you to come into our lives and remained very much present in the moments where I could be aware of you. I even knew I was pregnant with you before the doctor confirmed it, because I felt you inside of me...just as you often feel me as one with you even though I am now in spirit. You connect with my energy and are very aware of the love and experience of being one with me. The creative process is much the same in the sense where you must be connected in mind, body, and spirit to that which you want to experience.

You are creating moments in your life through this process, yet somehow when you need to introduce a new action and mindset into your creative process, it seems as if it is difficult and almost impossible to achieve. The truth is you are already using this process to create those experiences that you no longer wish to have in your life, now you can use the process to create those experiences that you do wish to experience. It truly is as simple as making the decision to carry out your goal through repeating new patterns in your life to replace the old ones. This is not impossible, this is what you do each and every moment except now you are empowering yourself in the process.

Understanding how you reach a destination is important in the journey and now you know how you create your life. This is to teach you that you can create positive experiences from negative ones, and love from fear. You cannot get more empowered than that! Do not fear what you don't understand Sophia, become empowered by it through knowledge and understanding. Every day we create our lives through being disconnected and numb to the world around us, even to the point where we have convinced ourselves that we cannot have what we want. How is it that we are so quick to lie to ourselves and believe an illusion? Yet when we have the choice to empower ourselves, we fail to recognize that we use the same creative process to bring experiences that bring us fear and love. It is just our choice as to which emotion we want or need to create at the moment.

So many of us convince ourselves that we cannot have what we want, only what we need because we choose not to connect ourselves to what we actually want. Connect your thoughts, emotions, and actions to that very thing you wish to experience in your life, and if you remain steadfast on that connection, you will see it created into your experience. Spend your moments being present and in the moment because this is the power of creation. When you are lost in thought and spend countless hours going through life on "auto-pilot," then you are creating through patterns that you have already established. Oftentimes these patterns no longer serve your greater good because they keep you "stuck" in the same experiences.

By connecting with the present moment at all times, you realize that you are in control of your thoughts, emotions, and actions, and can create deliberately through love. You can create good thoughts even when you are feeling emotions of frustration, just by changing your focus. When you are experiencing sorrow or fear, you can change shift your attention to being in an attitude of gratitude for the things and people in your life that bring you joy. This will help you realize that even though we cannot control what others do, we can always control how we react to the people and situations that affect us. Nobody will ever control your destiny if you always remain connected to the present moment.

Creating Through Body

Think about what it is that you want to create. Then pay close attention to how your body feels when you think about having that very experience in your life. If you want to win a beauty pageant, then think about winning the pageant of your dreams. Your body is composed of energy and your vibration will change with the excitement of having the pageant title. When you feel the shift in your energy, focus on how it feels in your body. Are you getting a surge of adrenaline or is your skin covered with chills from the excitement of having it? When you notice how your body feels, then continue thinking about the pageant win and try to grow your energy and the adrenaline surging through your body. Use this technique often throughout the day, so your body continually experiences the excitement of having the pageant win.

The more you create the sensation and the experience of that win, the easier it will be for your body to create it immediately. Soon, you will discover that you are experiencing the feelings of your body having that very experience you are trying to create. As you know, the very reason we desire to experience a goal is to feel the emotion and the energy through our body. It makes us feel good to create it, so we want to continue the feelings of having it. Just the experience of creating the feeling of your energy and the emotion of winning now before you even step foot on the pageant stage, brings the experience into your reality. Soon, your brain cannot tell the difference between what is real and what is illusion. From this comes the creation of that very experience that you have intended to draw into your life.

Creating through Emotion

By using the same method to change the energy of your body, you can create manipulating your emotions in the same manner to "trick" your mind into believing that the experience of winning your pageant has already happened. Remember that the goal of deliberate creation is about experiencing love on every level...mind, body, and soul. In order to control your life as much as humanly possible, you must be in control of your creative process. The problem lies when we forget that we are creative spirits having a human experience, and believe the illusion that we are humans creating our lives through the hands of fate.

When you become aware of your energy vibrating through your body through the creative process, you must also center your attention on what emotions you are experiencing with the creative process. Your emotions can be of excitement, joy, love, or anything that has a love based foundation. If you will connect the positive vibrations in your body with the feelings of love and joy, then you are adding one more element to manifesting your desired goal. Feel the emotions of joy while your body is experiencing its heightened senses and you are creating the experience of achieving your goal without seeing it into fruition yet. This is why it is so important to be aware of your thoughts and emotions on a continuous basis throughout the day. You can control what you feel just be creating the sensation of how your body feels when achieving your dream and what your emotions experience. By deliberately tapping into your creative process as often as you can throughout the day, you are in essence experiencing achieving your goal even before you manifest it into your reality.

Creating through action:

Finally when you add the element of acting in a way that supports your anticipated goal, then you are reaching the third and final process. Act as if you would if you already won the pageant title that you are trying to create in your journey. How would you dress every day? What would your appearance be from head to toe? How would you walk and carry yourself when you enter a room or meet a complete stranger? What would you stand for and how would you change the world? Would you use a blog or a website to come from a place of contribution and spread your message of hope and healing?

Allow yourself to dream big and follow that dream up with action! This is how people create miracles in their lives, by allowing themselves the courage to be authentic. You are a co-creator with God and yet daily you place limits on yourself and your potential. You cannot set limits on what God is capable of, so as a co-creator with the Divine, how do you place limits on yourself? Would you look God in the eye and say that only half of the whole has complete divinity? Yet you do this each and every moment of your life that you pray to God to create miracles in your life, yet tell him in the same breath that you cannot "show up" for the creative process. What arrogance then we have that we follow that up with blaming Him for not completing the process.

Dear God, this world is filled with dreamers who have chosen to relinquish their power to create dreams and have become unbelievers because they choose not to have faith. If you have faith in God then you must complete the process by believing in yourself. For God cannot open a door that through Free Will, you choose not to place your hand on. You are co-creators, which means that you need one another to complete the process of creation. One cannot do it without the other, so always ask yourself if you are placing limits on God, because if you are then you are jeopardizing your goal by placing limits on yourself. God is not a part of your journey to be your journey – He is a part of you which makes Him a part of the process. You are responsible as well, so never fool yourself into believing something that is not true.

You are acting on Free Will each and every moment of your journey, and in that process you must be accountable to God for your part of the creative process...period! How many times will y hear in your lifetime, people complaining that they cannot achieve a set goal because it is not God's will? God's will is often your will, yet you act on fear and choose not to carry out your part of the journey.

Sophia, allow me to make you truly understand that although we are co-creators with God... we are not God. Ultimately our Creator knows more than we remember when we set out to complete this journey through life. We cannot play the Director of the movie that we have not written the perfect script for. Our role is to be present in the moment each and every day and contribute our best through mind, body, and soul, to experience the best journey of life possible. Although I got sick, I know your prayers for my healing were heard but I too had free will to pass when I felt I needed to go home again. Your prayers could not control my journey, and I know that is one of the hardest lessons as you struggle through the meaning of my illness.

What I want for you to gain from your loss of me is that you cannot control another person or situation outside of you. However you can control how you act and react to these situations and people, and I ultimately want you to gain power from this experience and know that you still have the ability to create a life out of love rather than fear. I see you every night as you struggle to pray for healing, because a part of you has lost faith in the power of prayer. I see the energy fading from your prayers and this is why I have chosen to guide you through your healing process. Can you even imagine the power that love has to transcend beyond what the eyes can see and the mind can perceive?

This same God that you prayed to for hope and healing is the same Creator that has allowed the process of life after death to transpire. Yet you blame Him for not listening and yourself for not believing enough. The best gift I can offer you is to own your power once again as you heal through this difficult grieving process. Own your power to create and your right to experience truth. Spend every moment in awareness throughout your days, creating and feeling – creating and feeling, and soon you will be a master at the art of creating! Enjoy the process and the journey. I am so proud of you, and always know that I am only a thought away.

I love you forever,

Momma

We Are All Connected
Chapter 11

As the weeks passed and turned into months, Sophia found comfort in the moments where she could focus more on her activities and take solace in her collection of letters that she had discovered written by her mom. Although she couldn't explain their appearance in her life, she cherished the fact that through these lessons, she was gaining strength and learning to cope once again. Sophia still had not shared her letters with her dad because she didn't want to risk losing the magic. Even though she had considered that her dad was writing these letters and leaving them in inconspicuous places where she would find them, Sophia still could not explain the fact that each of these letters were written with her mom's handwriting.

Because Sophia's mom wanted to be cremated, the ritual of visiting her gravesite was not an option for Sophia. Instead, she and her dad celebrated her life through visiting the beach that Grace loved so much. Some of the greatest memories that Sophia had of her mom was walking along the beach while talking about their goals and dreaming about life. The sounds of the crashing waves along the coast along with the melody of the seagulls brought Sophia's mind back to happier times. As she stared off to the ocean horizon, Sophia became lost in the freedom of peace that the ocean sounds brought her. She didn't even realize that an elderly man had taken his seat on the bench next to her.

As he slowly relished the ice cream cone he had in his hand, Sophia was slightly agitated that he would sit in her personal space and distract the joy she was experiencing that was long overdue. As Sophia glanced over to this gentleman, she noticed that he was wearing a gray suit with a tailored white shirt. She realized that this very distinguished man was dripping melted ice cream down the front of his jacket. "Sir, let me help you," she said as she quickly pulled tissues out of her purse and handed them to the man sitting next to her. He smiled at her and slowly wiped the front of his suit, but the ice cream continued to drip so he began to chuckle. "Millie, my wife would get so mad that I would eat ice cream in my favorite suit," he said. Sophia smiled back at him as she watched him pull out a cloth handkerchief from his suit jacket and wipe his chin.

"Would you like some ice cream?" he asked as he offered to buy Sophia an ice cream cone from the vendor who was parked nearby. "No thank you," Sophia replied as she watched her dad walking back up the beach towards her. "I think we're going to eat dinner soon, and Daddy never appreciated me eating dessert for dinner." The old man laughed and quickly began finishing off his cone. "I won't tell if you don't," he replied and for the first time Sophia saw a light flickering from his eyes. Although he appeared to be old in age there was something about his spirit that was very childlike.

He reached over and extended his hand to Sophia and said, "My name is Albert." Sophia returned the handshake and as she touched his hand Sophia noticed that his skin was warm and tender. It didn't reflect his age but felt very soft, as if his hands were the skin of a baby but the appearance of an elderly person. "I'm Sophia," she responded as she noticed his hand trembling as he pulled it away. Albert caught Sophia's attention on his hands and said nonchalantly, "I may not be as stable when I stand or walk, but I have the foundation of a 24 story building. Don't allow the obvious to deter you from the truth," he said.

Sophia looked at Albert and smiled warmly at him, as she was embarrassed that she was starting noticeably at him and wondered what her mom would think as she raised her with better manners than that. Sophia looked down at her lap and heard Albert chuckle again, this time it turned into a deep and jolly laugh and he leaned in towards her. "Don't worry ladybug," he said. "Not everyone gets my sense of humor either." Sophia looked quizzically at him, and asked, "Why did you call me ladybug?" Albert smiled at her and replied, "I have spent my entire life proud of the fact that I had the memory of an elephant. Lately I haven't been able to remember people's names, so I associate them with animals, flowers, anything that will help me remember them. You remind me of a ladybug," he said.

As Sophia listened, she grew more intrigued of Albert as he continued, "You have a very hard shell which you use to protect yourself, but also have a very colorful personality that you allow to shine through in your smile and your beautiful eyes. Ladybug, something in your life has caused you to hide underneath your hard exterior but whatever it is, you are a young lady underneath a hard shell, yet have all the colors of the rainbow in your spirit and you can connect with so much light around you." As Albert spoke Sophia found herself suddenly connected to this elderly man who she had just met moments ago.

After finishing the last of his ice cream, Albert turned his attention to Sophia who was staring off at the ocean where she seemed to lose herself in the ease of the waves that somehow soothed her soul. He studied her and noticed the small dimples that accented her cheeks, and thought how beautiful this young girl's smile was in the few times he was able to see it during their conversation. "Ladybug," Albert interrupted as Sophia turned her attention back to him. "What's your dream?" Taken aback from Albert's question, Sophia smiled and shifted uncomfortably on the bench. "Everyone has a dream," he continued "and someone as young as you are must be filled with them."

Sophia looked down at her sandals and began searching her mind for anything she could come up with but drew a blank. As she shook her head, Albert continued "Of course, you have to be filled with dreams ladybug. You have your entire life ahead of you and mine is coming to a close." Sophia searched Albert's eyes and saw a smile form around his thin lips. As he chuckled, he said "I know I'm no spring chicken and my time is running short, and even at my young 92 year old age I have many dreams. One of which is to stay awake long enough to watch the sunset. You see, I was married to the love of my life for 65 years until the good Lord called her home. Amelia was the first girl I ever fell in love with and when she passed away I wanted to go with her."

Sophia stared at Albert as he looked off to the horizon recalling the memory of his late wife. "We knew each other so well that there were times we didn't even have to speak and we still knew what we were thinking. She knew me well enough to know that I can't match my socks and I knew her well enough to know that she deliberately bought me all the same color socks so I wouldn't walk out of the house with two different colors of socks on." Sophia and Albert both laughed and she watched as he continued looking out beyond the ocean waves and into the horizon.

Albert never turned his attention to her as he continued speaking, "before my Amelia passed away, I promised her that I wouldn't even think about passing on with her until I saw the sunset in the horizon. She knew that I grow sleepy very early in the day, but every day I sit on this park bench with an ice cream cone, and try to stay awake long enough to watch the sunset so I can give myself permission to go to Amelia when I fall asleep."

Sophia heard herself asking Albert before she even had the chance to stop herself, "What kind of a dream is that?" As she caught his eye, she suddenly felt ashamed and embarrassed that she had shown such lack of respect to a nice man whom she just met. Albert burst into laughter and focused his attention on her and said, "at least it's a dream ladybug. There are so many people who walk through their whole life completely oblivious to what they want. I want to enjoy a sunset that I have not gotten to see since I became sick and stuck in a hospital room for months. As I stared out the small window that overlooked another building, I promised myself that I would see a sunset after I got discharged. Well, I busted out of that joint and here I am sitting and waiting for my sunset."

Sophia found herself laughing uncontrollably at Albert's comment and found herself growing more and more comfortable with this man. "Ladybug, you have to find your dream. Even if it is to get through the day and see your sunset, or if it's as grand as being the best ballerina you can become. Find your dream and let it carry you through the toughest moments of your life. As you conquer those moments and your dreams, they will continue to change and carry you through this journey we call life. So ladybug...what's your dream?" Sophia took a deep breath and looked out at the sun that was starting to set across the horizon.

"I don't know," she replied as he remained silent. "I think my dream is to feel happy again, maybe even enter another pageant so I can start working on myself again and not feel so sad all of the time." As Sophia spoke, Albert watched her and noticed a very sad young girl behind those eyes. "Ladybug," he replied..."everybody needs a dream, especially during the moments of their life when they are feeling the lowest. It's our dreams that lift our spirits and ads hope to our broken heart, yet that is often the time when people disregard their hope and dreams because they don't believe they have the energy to accomplish them. People often look at life backwards and believe they need to be inspired to accomplish a dream when in fact they will become inspired once they take the plunge and commit themselves to creating their own dream."

Sophia caught herself nodding in agreement and realized that Albert was a very wise man, almost far beyond his 92 years. There was something about him that Sophia felt extremely comfortable with, and despite the fact that she just met him, she felt as if she had known Albert her entire life. Albert asked Sophia, "what do you hope to accomplish being in a beauty pageant? After all, you're pretty enough to win it ladybug but what is the overall experience that you want to create for yourself?" This question took Sophia by surprise and she realized that Albert asked a very legitimate question, and since there could only be one person to take home the crown in the pageant she needed to create an overall experience that she could control with or without the crown.

After pondering the question for a moment, Sophia responded. "I guess I want to know what it feels like to have a goal again, something to take my mind off of just being sad and put my energy into creating something good. Being in a pageant would force me to eat enough because I have lost my appetite and my dad is worried about me losing too much weight. Pageantry would also support my goal to focus on someone else besides me because we have to do community service. I don't know though if I have the strength because sometimes all I want to do is sleep and I am always so tired."

Albert nodded as he stared off into the sky which was turning a vivid shade of oranges, reds, and yellows. A smile crept across his face as he folded his hands and placed them on his lap. "Ladybug, you must always find the strength to care for yourself mind, body, and soul. How do you think I was able to make it all these years? After all, I wasn't born looking this handsome," Albert chuckled. "I had to take care of myself, especially after I lost my Millie. There has never been, nor will there ever be a woman more beautiful than my wife. I miss her." Albert's voice trailed into a soft whisper as he said that and Sophia could see his bottom lip tremble and his eyes fighting back the tears. He picked up the white cotton handkerchief once again and wiped his eyes with his quivering hand.

"How do you do it Mr. Albert,?" Sophia asked. "How do you manage to get up every day and get out of bed, brush your teeth, and eat knowing that it is taking every ounce of strength that you have?" Albert smiled and Sophia and gently patted her hand, "at first it wasn't easy." He replied, "Well except for the brushing my teeth part because I don't have any." Sophia started to laugh and he squeezed her hand underneath his. Sophia was surprised how soft his hand was since he was such an old man, but she appreciated the tender touch. "I prayed a lot Sophia, especially the first few months after I lost my beautiful bride. Soon I realized that as the weeks turned into months, I was breathing easier, crying less, and remembering more."

A tear fell slowly down Sophia's cheek as she stared off into the ocean waves and listened without looking at Albert. "I also realized ladybug that I could still feel my Millie around me so I would talk to her every day. Although she couldn't answer me in the way that I was used to, there were still moments that I swear I could hear her voice. Yes, ladybug my wife found a way to boss me around even from the other side." They both smiled, and Albert continued, "I learned that we are never alone and that our bodies create the separation but our souls always continue growing together through love."

Sophia looked across the horizon at the beautiful sunset that had formed while they were talking. She smiled ear to ear and said, "look Albert... there's your sunset. God saved the best one for you, it's so beautiful!" Just as she said those words, Sophia looked over to her side where Albert had been sitting on the park bench next to her. Albert was gone, as if he had disappeared while she was talking to him. Sophia jumped to her feet to look around for any sign of Albert and saw nothing. She felt her hand where Albert had been holding her hand and her skin was still warm from his touch, but where did he go?

"Albert?" Sophia called out as she noticed her dad walking slowly towards her, waving as he approached. "Who are you looking for Sophia?" Albert asked as he dusted off the sand from his shorts. "Albert," Sophia replied. "I wanted you to meet him but he just...disappeared." Sophia's dad looked puzzled then said, "Is Albert someone you were talking to on the telephone?" Sophia looked shocked at his line of questioning and replied, "No Daddy, he is the older gentleman who was sitting next to me for the past 15 minutes talking to me about sunsets...he even nicknamed me ladybug."

Sophia's dad looked surprised then worried. "Sophia I have been watching you from that umbrella since you sat down on the bench, and during that time you were completely alone." As a surprised Sophia began to question her dad about what he thought he saw, she looked down at the park bench where they had both been siting. Lying on the wooden bench was a crisp white cotton handkerchief, and as Sophia lifted the cotton hankie she noticed that underneath was a small pink envelope. Shocked and confused Sophia picked both the envelope and the hankie from the bench and slid them both into her pocket.

"Is everything alright?" her dad asked as Sophia struggled to understand the events that just occurred. She nodded slowly as she continued looking around at the active people walking and skating on the sidewalk, all the while looking for any sign of Albert. "Yes dad," she responded, "I'm fine." Still concerned but not wanting to make a big deal out of her questioning if he had seen anyone sitting next to her, Sophia's dad suggested they get some ice cream. "I heard they have the best ice cream here," he said. Sophia whispered under her breath, "So did I."

After the trip home, Sophia and her dad enjoyed a bite of take home pizza and she excused herself to go up to her room and clean up. As Sophia sat on the bed, she pulled the cotton handkerchief and pink envelope from her pocket. The front of the envelope were the words, Sophia Rose written once again in the same handwriting as her late mom. Sophia pulled the letter out of the envelope and slowly began to read it.

My Dearest Sophia,

We are all Connected

I have learned that the illusion of separation is one of the biggest illusions we have told ourselves. You live in a world, and experience of life trying to convince yourself of so many things that are not true, and the perception of separation is one of the greatest lies we tell ourselves. Separation is not real... but the feeling of it is very real in your experience. Remember in lesson two, where I told you that almost everything is an illusion? The illusion of separateness is among the top of that list of inaccuracies that we learn from others from a very early age. Let me start at the very beginning to see if I can explain this to you in the manner where your young mind will easily understand.

The beautiful truth is that as a young girl, you are probably more willing to comprehend this truth better than many adults. Children come into this experience of life still aware of their connection to the "other side" because they are so young. You see Angels and Spirit Guides and enjoy their company, and the adults around you label it as having "imaginary friends," whereas many of those imaginary friends are more reality than illusion. As you grow older and become more influenced by the opinions and fears of the world around you, children learn to adapt and conform to their environment so they begin to believe that nothing exists outside of what the eyes can perceive.

Throughout this process, many of your beautiful souls stop communion with God and stop believing in Angels and Spirit Guides and so your lack of attention to them replaces your relationship to them with another. Oftentimes the replacement of these relationships leads you to cultivate more relationships with the same energy and before you are aware of it, you have stopped believing in Angels and Spirit Guides and have replaced their connection with the relationships with other people. Once this occurs it becomes more and more difficult to develop the relationship once again. Not because your Angels and Spirit Guides are no longer there, but because you choose to believe they are no longer relevant in your journey. Much of your life comes down to free will and the thoughts, emotions, and actions you wish to create.

Your Angels and Spirit Guides never go away, but it is your lack of attention towards them that makes them feel separate from you. Let me give you a perfect example of this was your very first best friend Emily, who you swore was going to be your only friend forever? Since Emily lived next door to us, it was easy to see her every day and cultivate a relationship with her. When you wanted to play, you walked next door and Emily was there to greet you. When you wanted to see each other, the fact that she was so close to you helped you and Emily develop a beautiful friendship that lasted for many years. You knew without a doubt that Emily was very real and having her as a friend made you feel good, so you continued growing your friendship with her.

When you discovered that Emily was moving, your world became shaken because you were so afraid that you and Emily were never going to see each other again. Remember what I told you? Emily will always be your friend as long as you continue growing your relationship, and even though you would not get to see her as often you can still talk to her every day. When she initially moved you both spoke to one another daily and then as the months progressed, you spoke less and less until you lost touch with one another.

Emily was still very much alive and living her life, but your lack of attention and awareness to her made you feel separate from her until you lost the connection all together. Your feeling of

119

separateness from Emily created the illusion that she no longer existed, but the truth is that Emily is still very much in existence, but your feeling of separateness created the illusion that she doesn't. One day if you decide to reach out to Emily, you have the choice to cultivate the relationship with her once again. Turn your illusion of being separate towards the truth that separation is a thought and an emotion, which you follow through in the power of creation through your action.

Now turn your attention back to the feeling of separateness with your Creator and His Angels and Spirit Guides that are always present in your environment. Although you may have stopped communicating with them and cultivating a relationship doesn't mean they are still not present and around you every moment of your life. Recognize that you have the power to create a special bond with them once again, except now you know that if you spend the days talking to them aloud then others may question you. Thoughts are heard and emotions are felt, and nothing separates us from the love of others, so connect with them through thought and emotion and take comfort that they are present with or without your awareness of them.

Sophia, it is important that you release the illusion of separateness because this will help you to continue growing your relationship with God. We are all connected because we are all energy only takes different forms. Look around you at the plants, animals, people and everything in your experience and know that you are as connected to these forms of energy as you are to God. You don't have to cultivate a relationship with everything around you, but you must honor and respect their presence and journey in their own life.

If you recognize that these words are from my heart and thoughts, then you are already feeling connected to me. I am not present with you in the physical form, yet I am still *communicating with you because I love you and nothing separates you from me. I have loved you from the moment I existed and before I even knew I was pregnant with you, because you and I have always been connected through love. Even though you have moments through your grieving that you feel very separate from me, trust that the feeling of my presence around you is as real as it was when you could see me.*

Nothing separates the love of a mother from her child, not in life and not in death. The spirit never dies, only the body and flesh grow weak from age or sickness. But since we are not our bodies then we continue to be very much alive in your thoughts and in your energy. I don't tell you this to frighten you but to bring comfort to you. Whenever you need me, think of me, or are even oblivious to me, know that I am always loving you and looking over you just as I was when I was alive and you could see me every day. I kissed your forehead and gave you a loving hug every day before you left for school and every night before you went to bed, and I still do this each and every day whether you are aware of it or not. Trust your intuition and when you sense my energy around you in moments when you need comfort, trust that I am still here to give you kisses from heaven. My energy still feels the same but since I am now in pure energy form, my touch may not feel the same.

I find you during moments of the day, touching your own forehead where I used to place kisses on you before school and in those moments, you are very aware of my presence. Then I notice your thoughts changing and allowing the voice of fear to create your illusion that you were just "imagining" things. Continue to pay close attention to your thoughts and emotions because they will continue to create your experiences throughout your life. Trust your heart and your intuition and never allow yourself to own another person's fear.

Because we are all connected, then understand the law of karma which states that whatever you do to another person, you have also done to yourself. Be kind to others, inspire others, empower others, and when you are feeling lack of any of these things, it means that you have not put enough out into the universe to reap your own inspiration and empowerment. If you are experiencing feelings of lack of inspiration, then see what you can do to inspire someone that your heart is leading you to inspire. Do this enough and you will be inspired beyond words! I am so proud of you and always know that I am just a thought away.

I love you forever,

Momma

Free Will God's Gift to You
Chapter 12

The next day Sophia came down for breakfast and saw her dad sitting at the table drinking a cup of coffee. Although she never liked the taste of it, Sophia loved the smell of fresh brewed coffee. "Good morning Daddy," Sophia said as she planted a kiss on his cheek and started rummaging through the empty cupboards for cereal. Sophia had not eaten breakfast since her mom passed away so there was no reason for her dad to keep the cupboards stockpiled with cereal. A shocked expression appeared on her dad's face as he watched his daughter open cabinet door after cabinet door. "What are you looking for?" he asked.

"I'm hungry," Sophia replied as she turned her attention to the refrigerator that also resembled the same empty shelves as the cabinets. Sophia's dad shuffled his newspapers around as he dropped them on the table and moved quickly towards the refrigerator, just hoping to find anything edible to make Sophia before she lost her appetite again for another several months. As he scolded himself for not being more diligent about keeping Sophia's favorite foods available, he quickly pulled out some ingredients to make his self-proclaimed *world's greatest pancakes.* As they both made breakfast together, Sophia felt as if some small amount of normalcy was beginning to enter their lives, and for the first time in months she thought that they may just get through this ordeal together.

Sophia searched for the right time to share with her dad her desire to enter a beauty pageant because she wasn't sure how he would respond. Although her mom had always been supportive of Sophia's dream to one day win a pageant, her dad was not the biggest fan of pageants because he never wanted Sophia to define her beauty through another person's eyes. "Daddy, I was thinking...that maybe ... I want to enter a pageant." As Sophia heard herself say these words, they seemed foreign and she was anxious about how her dad would respond. He stopped eating, looked at Sophia for several seconds, and said, "Why do you want to be in a pageant honey?"

Sophia looked down at her lap and recalled the conversation she had with Albert when he told her that everybody needs a dream. "I think it will help me to focus on myself a little bit and help me," Sophia paused. "Help me start to feel normal again. I know I haven't been myself and I want to start feeling more in control again instead of spending everyday either at school or locked in my room." She searched her dad's eyes for any sign of what he was thinking at the moment, and then she saw him smile. He put his fork down and said, "what if you don't win honey? Do you think it will make you feel worse or do you think that you are strong enough to take rejection from a group of strangers?"

Sophia thought about that question long and hard and finally responded, "Momma taught me that I am supposed to define my own beauty and I know I am not the prettiest girl in town. But what I do know is that I feel in my heart if I don't try it then I might begin to settle for not having dreams anymore." Sophia's dad leaned over and hugged his daughter, and as he pulled back he said gently to her. "Sophia I will honor any dream you have as long as it is important to you." Sophia smiled and released a big sigh of relief because she now had something she could focus her energy on that would bring her even an ounce of joy. "Thank you Daddy," she said as she gulped down her breakfast and ran up to her room. "I need to get on the internet and see what pageant I want to enter."

I don't know the first thing about pageants Gracie, he thought. *What have you gotten me into?* As the beautiful face of Sophia's mom crossed his mind, he had to chuckle that now he would be considered a pageant dad and Sophia's greatest fan. Sophia's mom had once been in pageants when she was in high school and the photos that Sophia had of her mom posing in beautiful gowns she once designed and sewed herself was an image that Sophia cherished. Now more than ever before Sophia wanted to emulate her late mother and enjoy the journey through pageantry that her mom once had. If nothing else, it would enable Sophia to feel that she and her mom shared something like this in common.

As the weeks passed Sophia researched pageants, dresses, shoes, makeup, and everything else related to competing in a pageant. She began to get overwhelmed and as she stared at the pictures of the beautiful girls that wore the prestigious crowns in these different pageant systems, Sophia began to doubt whether or not she was ready to pursue this goal. The more she researched the more anxious she became, as Sophia realized that with many of these pageants came a responsibility to be a voice for a cause. As her heart became more nervous, Sophia suddenly began talking herself out of competing in a pageant and decided that she just wasn't ready.

She would however take Albert's advice and begin caring for herself more through healthy eating and slowly allow herself time to heal day by day. This news didn't disappoint her dad, because although he was prepared to hire the necessary people to help Sophia in this journey, he was also nervous that he wasn't prepared to watch her already broken heart get hurt once more. In time he knew she would ask him again and when she was ready mind, body, and soul, Sophia would enter the right pageant for her at the right time. Meanwhile he was relieved that she was starting to show signs of healing.

Knowing that she would have to be connected to a cause and a charitable organization, Sophia began looking into charities that she thought one day she may want to be a part of. One afternoon Sophia came across a charity that supported breast cancer research and the home page of the website brought a sinking feeling to her heart. *What am I thinking?* She thought to herself. *There is no way that I can talk about this to another person...not now, and not ever!*

As the realization came to Sophia that her dream of entering a pageant would be short-lived, she became disheartened. So much so that she gathered the information and photos she had been collecting of dresses and pageants and threw them in the waste basket that was on the floor next to her computer table. As she fell back on her bed and stared at the ceiling, Sophia felt the all too familiar pains of sadness flood her heart and overtake her body once again. Sophia felt defeated and wondered if she would ever feel happiness again.

When Sophia awoke, she looked at the clock and realized that she had fallen asleep for over an hour. Feeling as exhausted as she did before she fell asleep, Sophia pulled herself up and brushed her hair. Something her mom used to do for her at the end of the day when they would have time to share about the events that happened that day. Setting the brush down, Sophia noticed the binder filled with photos sitting on her vanity – the same binder that she had thrown away earlier before she fell asleep. As she grabbed the binder to throw it into the wastebasket once more, a small pink envelope fell out of it and landed near her feet. Sophia stared at the envelope long and hard and slowly bent down to pick it up. For a moment she thought that her dad may have found the binder and put it on her desk, but how did the envelope get there?

As Sophia looked at the envelope with the words *Sophia Rose* written on the front, she felt joy filling in her heart. Carefully,

Sophia pulled the letter out of the envelope and began reading…

My Dearest Sophia,

Free Will is God's Gift to You

When you attended Sunday school you learned about the concept of free will, but I want to ensure that you understand what this means. Before you were even born, your father and I decided that we would help build the foundation of your life before you were even three years old. The foundation of character, honesty, integrity, and values were of the utmost importance to us so you could create your life from a foundation of strength and truth, and continue expanding on those values as you grew older. Even though you are still so young, your choices are perceived as limited because there are certain things that you do not have a choice over. For instance, you have a set bedtime every school night, you have to attend school and cannot go out with your friends unless supervised by an adult.

All of these situations may appear as if you do not have free will because you have no control over our rules and guidelines. Since many people would define free will as the freedom of choice without the consideration of anybody or anything prohibiting your choice, then it may almost appear as if you do not have free will. Consider though Sophia that free will may go beyond the obvious and begin through those things that you do have control over. Although you cannot control what another person says or does, nor can you control external things outside of yourself, you still have a great deal of control over your life and I always want you to remember that.

When you control your thoughts, emotions, and actions, you literally take control over so much of your life and how you create your experiences. Even at your young age you see the effects of the world around you and believe they are causes when in fact they are effects created from another cause. For instance, when you fail to study and do your homework when it is assigned and your teacher surprises you with a pop quiz, through your eyes you believed the cause of your poor grade was that you were not able to study for the quiz. The truth is that the cause of your poor grade was not the lack of knowledge about the quiz, but the fact that you failed to study the assigned homework that week which would have more than prepared you for your quiz.

I am telling you this not to make you feel badly about yourself, but to empower you with knowledge so you can create more experiences of love in your life than fear. So much of today's world is filled with technology, and you are growing up in an age where your influence lies beyond your immediate family and friends. Because of this, you are being exposed to the opinions and thoughts of people across the world, and how you control your own thoughts, emotions, and actions will help you prepare for this age of technology. There are many benefits of growing up in this age of social media because you have the opportunity to learn so much with just the touch of your computer. Consider there are also many negative influences that you will also be exposed to and how you handle both the positive and negative effects will ultimately determine whether or not you create a life or love or fear.

Free will lies within your complete control, and embracing this truth will allow you the freedom to know that you can control how you act and react to people and events around you. For instance, you cannot control if somebody says something negative about you, but you can control how you react to it. Do you understand that your thoughts are energy and combined with your emotions they can create things? Remember that you are created from energy, and when you focus your attention and energy on a situation, you will bring that experience into your life. This is where free will is crucial for you to understand.

Control your thoughts, emotions, and actions and only focus your attention on those things which bring about your experiences of love and gratitude and you will bring more love and things to be grateful for into your life. Think about the memories that we created together, and when you begin to feel sadness and your heart grieves for the physical loss of me then apply this concept of free will. Your body and soul need to grieve my loss Sophia but don't allow yourself to drown in the sorrow of the grieving. Give yourself permission to cry, and go through all the stages of grief as long as you need to in order to heal your spirit and your heart once again.

But remember that when your soul begins to take comfort in the memories and you can get through the days without breaking down, it does not mean that you are forgetting me. This means that Gods love is mending your broken heart once again so you can continue to remember me. Love and fear cannot coexist, so allow the memories to fill your mind when your heart begins to heal. Your thoughts, emotions, and actions will reflect your free will so be attentive to what you are thinking and feeling.

Control your thoughts and let them only focus on those things which will bring you more love into your life. Control your emotions which will harness the power of your energy and together with your thoughts, will lead to creating goals and experiences that you desire and will bring you more joy. Finally learn at a young age to control your actions, because they are the third step in the process of creation. You must remain in tune with your own energy and this will allow you to live your life through a proactive and deliberate experience, rather than just allowing yourself to be reactive in life.

When you create your experiences in a reactive manner, you are just reacting to the effects of the world around you, and this way of thinking will only allow you to stay in the "norm" of how everyone thinks and feels. Look around you and realize that so much of life is being created by experiences that others are reacting to. The more you react, the less you create and you are born of the Creator, and your ability to create your life is your gift from God. How you choose to create your life experience is your gift to yourself. I am so proud of you and always know that I am just a thought away.

I love you forever,

Momma

Everything You Do Matters
Chapter 13

In the next few weeks Sophia immersed herself in books studying the afterlife, and when she was not reading up on this topic, she was searching the website for more information on breast cancer statistics, research, and charitable organizations. As much as she wanted to deny it, she was beginning to believe in something greater than herself, and this hope was giving her something to sustain her. Whether it was that Sophia believed that the she could lift herself from this depression or trying to understand how her mom was somehow able to communicate with her from beyond, there was too many questions Sophia had that went unanswered.

Whether her dad was leaving Sophia these letters in hopes of healing her heart, or maybe her mom had written them before she passed away and left them for her dad to surprise her with, Sophia still couldn't account for the fact that she was finding the letters during the moments in her life when she most needed them, and what about Albert? Where did Albert go and how did he disappear so quickly? The fact that Sophia's dad didn't see him sitting next to her for nearly 15 minutes didn't make any sense. Nonetheless, Sophia found a distraction that was leading her out of her own misery and this was not something that she was going to take for granted.

Sophia realized this chain of events was the rope she needed to begin pulling herself out of the dismal depression she had been experiencing for so long. Getting a chance to focus her energy on finding ways to make a difference in the lives of other people became Sophia's primary mission. She studied more throughout the day so she could dedicate her evenings to researching the mystery of connections between mothers and daughters. Slowly Sophia's grade began to rise and she began to put on some of the weight she lost on her tiny frame. Although she still was not able to reconnect with many of her friends, she felt more comfortable being alone in her room and studying, researching, and learning.

As the months progressed, Sophia slowly began to rise above the pain of depression and she realized that it no longer hurt to breathe. One afternoon when Sophia was sorting through the collection of pink envelopes she had collected, she closed her eyes and for the first time began to pray. She wasn't sure how to begin this conversation with God since it had been months since she had prayed, having to admit that God only hears certain prayers and hers was not in line at the time.

God, Sophia prayed. *It's me, Sophia Bello.* She opened her eyes, took in a deep breath and thought to herself that this was a very awkward way to begin a conversation. *I know it has been some time since we have spoken. Oh sweet Jesus*, she thought as she opened her eyes and threw her palm to her forehead. Shaking her head, Sophia thought that this prayer thing was not going so well and as she lifted herself up from her knees, Sophia caught sight of a picture sitting on her nightstand of her and her mom hugging during a picnic. *I don't even believe that you will hear me*, she thought to herself.

Sophia put herself to bed and stared at the photo for several moments, as she recalled the beautiful day they had spent at the beach together. *God*, she prayed in silence, *if you can hear me I need your help. Please...hear my prayer.*

As Sophia closed her eyes she held on to the memory of her mom and called on that feeling that was building within her. *God, I don't know if I believe in you anymore*, Sophia prayed. *You are all I have and I need you.* As Sophia felt the connection to the yearning in her heart and the words escaping her mouth, she fell to the floor and began to cry. *God, I need you and I don't even know what to say to you. I know you hear me and feel me, and I can't... I can't feel you near me.* Sophia began to sob so uncontrollably that her body began to shake. *God, please hear me... I need you. I can't do this without you. Who am I to call on you? I don't know if I even believe you hear me, but I need you...please...*

Suddenly, Sophia felt a warm blanket of energy cover her entire body and envelope her like a glove. The euphoric feeling she had was so overwhelming that Sophia closed her eyes and laid in the feeling of love that was so powerful, she felt dizzy and as if her body was raising its own vibration ten thousand times over and she closed her eyes and relished in the familiarity yet strangeness of it. Sophia didn't want this moment to end and as she closed her eyes, she realized that she felt safer than she had ever felt before. Somehow in the feeling of this bliss Sophia felt safe and warm enough to fall asleep to the glow of the beautiful and magical energy.

When Sophia awoke later that night she was tucked into her bed with the blankets wrapped around her shoulders just like her mom used to tuck her in. Her arms were wrapped into this blanket so tightly that she felt like she was in a cocoon and in the safest and warmest place in the world. Sophia didn't want this feeling to vanish, so she closed her eyes again and just felt the bliss of the warmth of the blanket, the safety of her nest, and the love that lingered from the moments of her prayer.

Father God, she prayed again except this time she felt the words resonate within her spirit as strongly as she felt the love and warmth from the blanket and energy that was magically swirling around her. *I'm sorry that I lost faith in you, but I lost faith in myself and everything I ever believed in. I don't know why you said no to my prayer and took momma home when you said yes to my friend Megan's mom who had breast cancer and is home with her family. I don't know if you loved momma more or Megan's mom more, but all I do know is that I can't do this alone. I need you...please help me.*

Once again Sophia felt comforted by the loving energy that covered her and she closed her eyes and continued praying. *Please give me a sign that momma is in heaven with you, anything that will let me know without a shadow of doubt that she is sitting on your lap looking down on me. I've been getting letters and I don't know if momma left them for me before she died, or if Daddy is writing these, but if they are really from momma then please give me a sign. I need to believe in you again and I need to hope that I will see her again, but most importantly I need to know that you love me and that I'm not as alone as I feel. Stay with me and continue to comfort me while I fall asleep.*

As Sophia began to fall asleep once again in the bliss of the warm energy and light she was experiencing, Sophia had a dream. Sophia was standing in a dark room and standing in front of her was her beautiful mom. She didn't speak to Sophia but stood smiling, and as Sophia looked closer she noticed that her mom was holding a red velvet robe and a jeweled scepter in her right hand. As Sophia began walking towards her mom, she realized that she was not standing in a dark room, but instead she was standing alone with her mom on a dark theatre stage.

Sophia suddenly awoke and smiled as she realized that her mom visited her, and this realization brought a smile to her face. Sophia had read stories of people who have lost loved ones and they appeared to them in dreams, and now she realized that she had received validation from God that her mom was in heaven. As Sophia pushed herself up from bed, she relished in the feeling of comfort and love. For the first time since her mom passed away, Sophia felt her mom's presence and energy and knew without a doubt that this "dream" was in fact a visit.

Later that morning Sophia went to breakfast with her dad because she was finally getting her appetite back and the idea of pancakes lifted her spirits. As they sat in the quaint restaurant, a lovely young woman with blonde curly hair approached them. "Good morning," she chirped as she pulled out a writing pad and asked, "I'm Stephanie, can I take your order?" Sophia's dad didn't hesitate as he ordered the largest breakfast combination on the menu and topped it off with hot coffee. Sophia giggled as Stephanie made a comment about the fact that he must be hungry then she turned her attention to Sophia, and said, "what about you sweetheart?" she asked. As Sophia began to order, the Stephanie stopped writing and stared at her for a few seconds; just long enough to make Sophia nervous.

"I'm sorry," the Stephanie explained, "but you look so much like someone I used to know." Sophia smiled and continued to order, but still Stephanie stared at her without writing her order on the pad of paper in her hand. Sophia stopped talking and looked nervously at her dad who was now getting uneasy himself. Stephanie looked down at the table embarrassed, and tears began filling her eyes. She looked back at Sophia and said, "You look just like someone who made a huge difference in my life. You see, she used to come here a lot and sit at my station every day and have a cup of coffee. This beautiful woman would tell me every day that I was pretty…something I had never heard from anyone before. Not only that, but she told me I was smart and convinced me to go back to school and finish my degree. I am attending night school and just work here during the days so I can pay for my tuition until I graduate."

Stephanie continued talking as she picked up the pad to write down Sophia's order. "What was so amazing about this woman is that she was a teacher and she made me feel smart enough to believe in myself again. I haven't seen her in a few months, but when I do I want to tell her that I am getting the last few credits I need to earn my degree and become a teacher...just like she was." Sophia's smile disappeared as she looked at her dad who was giving her the same expression. "What was this woman's name," he asked. "Grace," she replied. "I nick named her amazing Grace because she was an Angel to me. God put her in my life so I could believe in myself again and become a better version of myself. She didn't know me from Adam but she took the time every morning for several weeks to make a difference in my life." As she finished taking their order, Stephanie smiled and said she would be right back with more coffee and hot chocolate for Sophia.

Slowly Sophia looked up at her dad who was watching Stephanie walk away and turn their order in. "Daddy?" Sophia said, "Do you think she was talking about momma?" Sophia's dad turned to her and shook his head in uncertainty. "I don't know honey," he said as he observed Stephanie walking back to their table with a coffee refill in one hand and a large mug of hot chocolate underneath a mound of white, fluffy whip cream. "Tell me more about Grace," he said as Stephanie carefully placed the beverages down being careful not to spill them.

"She was beautiful both inside and out," Stephanie continued as she put her hands in her pockets. "I had shared with her that I dropped out of school years ago when I was so close to completing my college credits. With life getting in the way, I always wanted to go back but just didn't think I could cut it again at my age. Well, this teacher talked to me about opportunities that were available to help me afford school and suggested that I look into them. One day she brought me a list of available grants and websites that I could research so I could apply and I was able to get one. Between working during the day and the grant money I was able to get, I have been attending school and am finishing my degree. I owe it all to her."

Sophia's smile returned and she looked at her dad, "it's her Daddy." Sophia said, "I think it's momma who helped her." Just as her dad began explaining to Sophia that it may just be a coincidence, Stephanie's expression changed and she pulled her hands out of her pocket and knelt down next to Sophia. "My God," she said, "you're her… you're Sophia Rose." Just as Sophia began to nod, Stephanie reached out her hand and placed it on Sophia's. "Do you know how much your mom loved you? She was so proud of you and she could not share with me enough how you were her greatest accomplishment."

Stephanie's eyes filled with tears as she listened to Sophia and her dad explain to her that Grace had lost her battle to cancer and passed away. She listened intently as they described the last several months of Grace's life, and they were so honored that they came to the coffee shop and got to hear Stephanie's story. As they finished their breakfast, Sophia and her dad shared their excitement about their chance encounter with Stephanie and both felt a sense of pride that Grace was able to impact another person's life to the extent that she did, without even knowing Stephanie.

As Stephanie placed the ticket on the table, she explained how happy she was that she got to meet them both and told Sophia again how much she resembled her beautiful mother. As Sophia's dad excused himself to pay for the meal at the register, Stephanie looked thoughtfully at Sophia. "You have the same light in your eyes that she did," Stephanie said. "I know she was very proud of you." Just then Stephanie reached into her pocket and handed Sophia a small pink envelope with the words *Sophia Rose* written on the front. "She asked me to give this to you," Stephanie said. "You see, one of the last times I saw your mom, she asked me to do one favor for her without questioning her. She said that one day a young girl would come into this diner and she would look like a mini version of herself. I promised her that when I knew for certain that you were the intended recipient of this letter then I would give it to you when nobody else was watching. She never told me why she wanted me to give it to you, because I never knew she was sick. Your mom just asked that I keep this letter with me at all times until the day came when I would meet you."

As she handed Sophia the envelope Stephanie smiled and said, "Your mom was and continues to be a very special person. It was truly a pleasure getting to meet you Sophia and I will keep you and your family in my prayers. God bless you." Before Stephanie turned to walk away, she smiled at Sophia and gave her a little wink. "You are a very special girl Sophia Rose," she said as she walked away.

After breakfast Sophia and her dad walked along the beach, throwing seashells and feeding seagulls some of their left over breakfast toast. She wanted so badly to read the letter Stephanie gave her, but knew it was important to wait until she was alone because she didn't want to have to explain this or the other letters she received. The chance meeting with Stephanie made Sophia smile and feel very special that her mom impacted a stranger who returned the favor by holding onto a letter for months in the event that she met Sophia.

After they got home Sophia ran upstairs to her room and closed the door. She pulled the letter out of her pocket and sat down on the bed and began reading.

My Dearest Sophia,

Everything You Do Matters

One of the biggest misconceptions that we choose to convince ourselves of in this journey through life is that we are insignificant. From birth we are taught to believe that nothing we do matters and that we are all victims of fate. This false belief is often confirmed through events happening in the world outside of us, and through relationships that we encounter daily that negate our worth. We then go through life trying to become invisible because we feel invisible, How is it that in a world populated with over five billion people, so many individuals walk through their life feeling isolated and alone? What's worse is that in the process, we alienate ourselves from Source energy who resides within us.

When you feel alone and isolated from everyone and everything around you, the world begins to look much smaller and we choose to notice those experiences that reinforce our feelings and thoughts. If you feel sad or lonely, then you often choose to recognize people in school or events that take place that confirm you feeling sad. If you feel isolated from God and disconnected from love, then you tend to withdraw and primarily notice those people who make you feel alone and disconnected from love. Society feels so badly about themselves, that they try to convince others around them that they should feel insignificant and unimportant as well.

My child, this is such a false belief and if you could see what I see, then you would realize what a true vision of perfection you are! We are each created from our Maker and God has no beginning and no end which means Source is pure energy. Energy creates everything around you, so if you are co-creating your life experience with God then everything you do throughout your life matters. Your choices matter to you if you decide at a young age to expose yourself to negative influences through people or experiences on the internet. Everything you do matters when you are struggling through your young life attempting to understand that you are the only voice of approval you actually need. Everything you do matters when your choices create a foundation of how your life is experienced and through those experiences, you define success.

Think about the people you choose to spend your time with and expend your energy on. When you are influenced by those who seek to help you grow into the greatest version of yourself, what you do when you are around them feels authentic. You know that your actions and intentions follow those which you know you would be proud of when you are looking me in the eyes and knowing we are connecting soul to soul. You also know that you are proud of what you would report back to me at the end of the day when you close your eyes and speak to me with the words, "Oh momma, I miss you so much...can I tell you about my day today?"

Remember that everything you do matters to you....this is one of the most important lessons you can understand, because you come into this journey through life to experience life for you and only you! Somewhere in the midst of listening to all of the lost souls around you, the truth gets lost and you become convinced that you are here to co-create your experiences for another. Not true! Your choices matter because they first and foremost matter to you... the co-creator of your life, so be very aware and responsible for your thoughts, emotions, and actions and pay careful attention to your choices. They will be a part of your life throughout your entire journey so be sure that you are serving your greater good with each and every decision and action that you take.

Listen first and foremost to yourself and your instinct, because God speaks to you through your thoughts and emotions and *when you honor yourself then you honor you co-creator. Life then becomes a celebration rather than just a chore, and if nothing else, realize that at any instant you can alter the course of your life by altering your thoughts, emotions, and actions. I am so proud of you and the woman that you are becoming! I am so proud of you and always know that I am just a thought away.*

I will love you forever,

Momma

Understanding Reality
Chapter 14

The more research Sophia began doing on pageants, the more she realized that she was going to have to prepare for her competition in the same manner that she prepared for tests at school. Sophia realized that pageantry wasn't about just looking pretty in a dress, but it was about community service, excellent grades, and overall communication with individuals as well as in front of an audience of 1000 people. Sophia began to understand why so many of her friends who competed in pageants were so involved in areas of their life that allowed them to become better versions of themselves.

She would talk to her dad about areas of pageantry that she liked and areas that she didn't feel as confident in, and her dad would listen and let her share her thoughts. Sophia appreciated him allowing her to express her concerns and her fears without judging her. She shared with him that in the pageant she wanted to compete in, there were platforms or causes that each delegate got to choose to promote throughout her reign. As Sophia tossed out several platform ideas she considered such as bringing awareness to animal cruelty and neglect, promoting healthy eating, and the more she talked the more quiet her dad became.

Finally as she finished taking a breath, Sophia stopped talking and looked at her dad to read his expression. She wasn't able to understand what he was thinking, so she remained silent and waited for him to break his silence. Finally after what seemed like forever to Sophia, her dad finally spoke. "Sophia," he said, "what about having your platform revolve around breast cancer awareness." Taken by surprise, Sophia looked down at her feet and thought about what he said. Although she had considered this as a platform, she was terrified because she didn't know if she had the strength to talk about something that nearly broke her.

"I don't know Daddy," Sophia replied. "What if I'm not strong enough to talk about this without crying? Sophia's dad looked at her with the kindest eyes and replied, "Sophia this journey is about you and you alone. So if you are not ready, then now is not the time to talk about it. When the time is right, then it will all fall into place...what about raising awareness about animal neglect? After all, you love animals and all of our dogs have come from the animal shelter, so you can raise money for them and feel like you're making a difference at the same time."

Sophia liked this idea because she did love animals and knew that she would enjoy working more with the animal shelter. She already volunteered her time once a week to walk the dogs, so she would talk to the manager of the shelter and get some ideas of how she can get more involved. The more Sophia thought about getting immersed with the shelter, the more excited she became. This community service idea was going to force Sophia to focus on something other than herself, and this idea alone was motivation enough to get involved. Sophia was so tired of dealing with the up and down cycles of grieving, and she wanted to begin taking control of her life, but wasn't sure how.

Maybe this opportunity to enter a pageant would help her find a way to start controlling her goals, make new friends, and do something from contribution along the way. As Sophia emailed the pageant director for more information, she felt a sense of relief and excitement. A smile crossed her face as she looked at the photo of her and her mom sitting on a park bench at her favorite beach. The memory of this photo brought joy to her as she recalled the fun they had enjoying an afternoon of girl time.

Sophia treasured those memories and her biggest fear was that she would begin to forget what it felt like to be around her mom. Sophia set the photo down and stared at the photo for several seconds as she realized that the park bench that they were sitting on was the same park bench that Albert was sitting on next to her when he suddenly vanished into thin air.

The tap on the door startled Sophia out of the daydream she was experiencing, and when her dad walked in to let Sophia know that he wanted them to go to the animal shelter to walk some dogs. As they walked into the shelter, the sound of barking dogs sounded like bells in Sophia's ears. She loved animals and her dad knew that the best way of getting to Sophia's heart was to get her out the door and into the shelter. As Sophia put a leash on a chocolate lab dog, she smiled and yelled that she would be back soon as she walked out the door.

The energy that this 60 pound dog possessed was almost too much for Sophia to control as she tightened the leash around her hand to ensure not losing her grip from his strength. "As she was able to regain control over the dog and begin walking him in tempo with her, Sophia was able to enjoy their walk and took pleasure in the way he sniffed everything around him especially the flowers. She had never witnessed an animal so enamored by the scent of flowers and every chance he had, this beautiful animal would stand in the flower bed and just flash an expressive grin.

Sophia enjoyed walking him and realized that he was now her favorite dog to walk, because the only other living creature she knew who enjoyed the scent of flowers as much as he did was her mom. As Sophia smiled at the lab, she turned to make her way back to the shelter but the lab wouldn't move. "Come on boy," she called out as she knelt down and patted her knee to get him to come to her but he stood still in his tracks. *Great*, she thought to herself. *I have to get the stubborn, flower loving dog that almost outweighs me.* Sophia walked over to the lab who was still giving her an expressive dog smile and she had to giggle. "I know you love these flowers, but we need to get back before they think I adopted you," she said as she gently pulled on his collar and began walking again.

The lab didn't move but stood his ground as he looked around then began smelling the flowers again. Feeling slightly exasperated, Sophia walked back over to him and watched as he laid down on some of the beautiful flowers. *Oh no,* she thought, *you are going to get us both in trouble.* As Sophia began pulling the dog to his feet, she overheard a friendly voice saying, "Your dog sure loves those flowers...do you need help?" Sophia turned around to see a friendly face of a man who she had seen volunteer at the animal shelter. "No sir," Sophia replied, "I think I have him."

Just then Sophia tripped over the leash and fell on top of some beautiful daisies next to where the lab was laying down. The gentleman laughed and extended his hand to Sophia, "I'm Tom and I think you might need a hand." As he pulled Sophia to her feet, he looked at the lab and made a whistling sound that encouraged the dog to quickly jump to his feet, and with a wagging tail walked directly to Tom. "How did you do that?" Sophia asked startled. "You just have to be stern but loving to him or he will lie in those flowers all afternoon. There is something about this flower garden that this old boy loves and every chance he gets to walk, he ends up directing his walker to this exact location. I don't know what it is, but he loves it."

Sophia watched as the dog licked Tom's face and tried to go back to the flowers to lay in them again. "You know," Tom continued, "animals have a keen sense of intuition...so do children. They sense energy around us that we don't necessarily see. There may be someone or something standing in this flower bed that attracts this dog here often. He has been with us for some time now because older dogs are generally harder to adopt, since so many people want puppies. He's a good boy, just loves flowers."

A smile crossed Sophia's face as she and Tom stood by the flower bed and observed the lab wag his tail and smell the flowers, as if he were enjoying them with an invisible friend. A puzzled expression crossed Sophia's face as she watched the dog and tried to understand what Tom meant about dogs sensing energy. "What do you mean that dogs can sense people or things that aren't there?" she asked as she looked up at Tom who was smiling and enjoying the playful lab. "We are all made from energy Sophia, everything that you see is energy. When people die in the physical sense, they are still very much alive because energy cannot be created or destroyed. Our spirit remains alive event though the physical body has shut down."

Tom and Sophia watched the lab without looking at one another, but Sophia was listening intently as Tom continued sharing his thoughts. "When people die, their spirits remain alive and sometimes they continue to watch over us and remain connected to us through those things that they loved. If they loved water, then you may sense their energy around you when you are walking along a beach or taking a bath. If you loved...flowers, then they may find it easier to connect to us through the love of flowers or in this case, roses." Tom began laughing as he watched the lab smelling the roses in the flower bed and pushing his nose into the velvet petals as if he were searching for something.

"Whatever this dog is sensing he is enjoying every minute of it because his tail is wagging and he appears to be smiling doesn't he?" Tom asked as Sophia nodded in agreement. "How do you know that he just doesn't love flowers?" Sophia asked as she waited for Tom's answer without even looking up at him as he replied, "that's because he is trying to tell you something ladybug." Sophia suddenly turned her head to look at the man standing next to her and her jaw dropped as she saw Albert standing where Tom once was. He was smiling and winked at her just as he did in the park before he suddenly disappeared. "Albert!" she shouted and suddenly the lab became spooked and began to run off.

Sophia chased him for a few steps and grabbed his leash, and as she turned around to talk to Albert once again, he was gone. "Albert?" Sophia shouted as she stood in awe wondering how he was able to move so quickly and hide from her. After all, Albert was not exactly a young boy but he moved like a stealth young man. "Albert?," Sophia called out once more and when she realized that he wasn't coming back, she noticed the dog standing once again in the flower bed. "What are you looking at?" Sophia asked in a whisper as she slowly walked towards him. Suddenly the scent of roses grew stronger and stronger, but she wasn't surprised since she was standing in a flower bed covered with roses. Something felt different suddenly Sophia began getting ice cold chills covering her entire body. The chills were immediately followed with an energy touching her face and as she stood motionless in the flower bed, Sophia began to cry. "Momma?" she said as she recognized the energy around her as the most familiar feeling she knew.

Suddenly Sophia was interrupted as her dad rushed up to her and took the leash out of her hands. "Sophia, are you hurt? What's the matter sweetheart? He asked as he pulled her into his arms and allowed her to weep. "Daddy I just felt momma near me," she cried. "I felt her touch my face." The more she heard herself talk the more she cried because she wasn't sure if she was starting to lose her sanity or if this experience along with the letters she was finding was in fact real.

As they drove home from the shelter Sophia shared with her dad everything that had been happening from finding the pink envelopes, to Albert disappearing, to the waitress at the restaurant giving Sophia the letter. Afraid that her dad would be mad at her for not disclosing this sooner, he listened silently then took a deep breath. "Sophia, I'm not sure what to think, but this I do know. Your mother loved you very much and I think she left a letter for me to give to you, so maybe she has done the same with others who she knew would find you."

Even as he spoke, Sophia's dad wasn't sure of this and felt guilty that he had no logical answer, but this was all he could come up with. "What about Albert?" Sophia asked. "He has appeared and disappeared into thin air and I can't figure him out." Again her dad was quiet and thought for a few moments." Well," he said carefully. "I supposed if you ever see him again you can ask him just that." Even that answer didn't make sense and Sophia's dad wished more than ever that her mom was around to deal with this. He was not sure if he was helping or adding more harm to this delicate situation.

After all, he was aware that grief can cause the mind to react differently and under enough stress it could make someone up. He only wished that Dr. Archer didn't suddenly leave because she was actually able to get through to Sophia and begin cracking that hard shell she had built around her for protection. Realizing the silence in the car, he looked over at Sophia as she said, "you don't believe me do you?" He shook his head and replied, "I didn't say that honey, I just think that there has to be a reasonable explanation and maybe when you see your friend Albert again you can ask him for one."

Sophia remained quiet as they walked back to the animal shelter as she realized that her dad was right. If she ever saw Albert again, she would ask him some very specific questions so she could prove to her dad that she wasn't crazy. "Meanwhile," he continued. "Tonight is pizza night, what kind do you want?" Sophia's attention went to the conversation as she got excited about their pizza and movie night. As Sophia removed the harness from the lab and began putting him back into his pen she noticed a small pink envelope taped to the front of the door with the words *Sophia Rose* written on the front.

Ensuring that the lab was securely back into his area, Sophia sat down in front of his crate and opened the envelope. Tucked neatly inside was a letter and as she opened the pages of the letter the scent of roses grew stronger and the lab even walked towards Sophia and began pawing at the door. With one hand she reached in to soothe the dog and pet his head, and with the other hand she held the letter and began to read.

My Dearest Sophia,

Understanding Reality

If you could see what I have discovered here on the other side since my passing, you would be astonished! Everything is so beautiful and the emotion of love is so magnified it is almost indescribable. The colors are so vivid and alive that it makes sunsets on your journey appear almost dulled and muted. Whatever you see in your journey through life is amplified on the other side because there is no illusion to dull the senses. The brightest yellows and reds appear as if they have a hue so vibrant that they illuminate from the frequency of energy – pure energy. The light that fills your eyes on your journey and allows you to see beauty all around you is so bright on this side that it creates an optical illusion of what your senses would perceive as a halo effect. Souls glow on this side and we see one another from a place of love, so the beauty and the majesty here is the greatest work of art you could ever imagine.

Thoughts are heard and felt, and the way we communicate with each other is through our thoughts and emotions. Prayers are heard this way as well, and whenever you are at a loss for words and are reaching out to God, know that your thoughts and feelings are heard just as powerfully as your words are. Joy surrounds us and everywhere we look there is beauty in all that we see. The greatest tool for communication is our energy Sophia, and we are transported instantly through our thoughts. This is why I am able to visit you in your dreams and connect with you in spirit, because I am now pure energy connecting with your energy through love.

Even though I have attempted to reach out to you so many times to let you know that I am fine, your sorrow and fear prevents you from believing that it is in fact me reaching out to you. Because of this, I have sent you butterflies and signs that only you would recognize to be my reaching out to you, but oftentimes your doubt disconnects us. This is why I come to you when you are sleeping my precious child. Because when you are asleep, there are no other distractions that can separate you from me; there is only love. I can lie next to you in your bed and allow you to feel the energy of my presence to let you know that I am here for you. Even though I am no longer in physical form, I am still very much alive through pure energy.

Those dreams that you have experiences with my visiting you at nights have not been dreams. They are actual visits from me, but since we are connected in energy then it is easier to come to you in thought and emotion, so you can be aware of my presence without being afraid or in doubt. You see when, you are deep in sleep and open to receiving my energy then it becomes easier to connect with you. When you awake, you question whether or not you have made these letters up in a fantasy in order to cope with my passing. The truth is that these letters are as real as I am! I will prove this to you once and for all, but only when you allow yourself to believe that your dreams and our connection through them are real.

As souls we come into this experience through life and convince ourselves that only those things that we see in physical form are real, and those which we cannot see are illusions. Oftentimes this is backwards thinking because reality exists in the mind – not the brain my child but in the mind, through our thoughts and emotions. We are not defined by our physical body any more than we are defined by our physicality. Our depth goes beyond anything measured, and reality lies within those things that we have a hard time understanding.

When I was still in physical form, you believed that I was very much alive and I was. But since my passing and transition from the physical form into the energetic form, it is more difficult for you to believe that I am still very much alive because your eyes *cannot see me other than in dreams. In these dreams, I don't speak to you but just smile at you and let you know that I am with you. These letters are another part of my energy that allows me to communicate with you without being physically present. If you consider the world you live in today, you have this type of communication accessible.*

When you send out an email to a friend and don't see that friend, but she responds back to you, then how do you know that the email is actually from her? When Jennifer moved from next door to Montana, then how did you know for sure that the emails you received from her were in fact from Jennifer? After all, you had not spoken to her in months yet you managed to stay in contact through email and texts on a daily basis. Your mind knew without a doubt that Jennifer was very much alive even though you were not able to physically see her.

Yet, you receive messages from me and are filled with doubt that I even still exist...why? Is it because your eyes can no longer see me, or because you are so filled with fear of the unknown that you refuse to embrace reality and remain in a state of illusion? As a child you walked by such strong faith, and you believed that anything was possible. Now you look at your beliefs and question everything you have ever believed about faith, love, and prayer, and try to convince yourself that none of this can be possible without actually seeing me.

Sophia, as you have discovered we are all pure energy and when you see me in your dreams, you also feel me as well. You sense the way my energy felt when you were once held in my arms and you oftentimes even smell my perfume or the scent of roses and wonder if I am near you. I am my child. I don't tell you this to frighten you but to bring you comfort in this time of healing for you. I visit your Daddy often as well, when he sits on his favorite chair and just stairs into the darkness, because like you, he misses me greatly. He just doesn't share that with you because he is trying to remain strong for you as well. His heart is broken and his faith too has been shattered because every prayer request he had was sent out for my healing.

When I grew sicker and he realized that my passing was close at hand, he became so closed off to prayer that he seldom prays anymore. What comfort he would have if he only knew the lessons you have been taught by me. But his heart is too closed off right now to be open to these words. Realize though that just as your heart was closed off, when the light can permeate his spirit again and he begins to allow healing into his spirit, you will say something to him that will enlighten him and will reignite a spark in his spirit once again.

Even though you are a child, you are wise beyond your years and a very old soul who has chosen to experience this life journey for the greater good of your own growth and the growth of others. Understand that with every experience you have in your journey, there is a bigger picture that you cannot yet see. A mission or larger goal that if you stay true to yourself and control your own life, you will uncover and experience love greater than the pain you have just experienced through my passing.

These words will serve to uplift you and make you aware of your greater journey my child, so stay true to yourself and you will remain on course for your calling. I am so proud of you and remember that I am just a thought away.

I love you forever,

Momma

The Balance of Power
Chapter 15

For the remainder of the day Sophia thought about the letter and who could have taped it on the crate, as many saw her leave to walk the dog but the letter was definitely her mom's handwriting. What was more confusing to Sophia was the fact that it mentioned her dad's grieving and not praying , and although she might be able to justify some of the letters before that may have been written prior to her mom's passing she could not understand how they were so relatable to what she was experiencing now.

As Sophia laid in bed that night she thought about her dad and how worried she was about him. Guilt overcame her as she felt selfish that she had not even asked him how he was managing to deal with the loss of his wife. When Sophia's dad came into the room to check on her before bed, she sat up and asked, "Daddy do you pray?" Taken aback from the question, he stood motionless in front of her for several seconds then slowly responded, "I used to." He sat on the bed next to Sophia and looked at the framed photo of his beautiful wife and daughter at the beach, then he asked "do you pray?"

Sophia looked down and chose her words carefully, "I do now. When momma died I stopped praying because I didn't think that God listened to me, or even cared about me. I stopped praying for a long time, but now I started to pray a little bit again." Sophia looked up at his face and stared into his eyes trying to search his thoughts through his expression. "What changed Sophia?" her dad asked as he smiled nervously at her.

"I started believing that momma is in heaven with God, and if she is then I should probably try to talk to him again."

As the expression changed on her dad's face, he looked down at her and touched her lightly on the cheek. "Sophia you remind me so much of your mother because she was a very spiritual woman as well. Sometimes our faith is all we have when we feel we have nothing left so never lose it. Faith is one of the most beautiful gifts to receive and one of the hardest to get back when we lose it." Sophia realized at that moment how hard he must be taking her mom's death. "Daddy, I'm sorry I never asked you how you were doing. I am so sorry that I didn't ask you once if you were alright."

He looked surprised to hear Sophia say these words, and then smiled at her so lovingly. "Sophia you were barely keeping your head above water, so never apologize to me because I am your father and supposed to be taking care of you — not the other way around." He embraced her and closed his eyes as he felt the anguish once again from the heartbreak of losing the love of his life. Whatever happened in his heart, he was certain to remain strong for Sophia and carry out the promise he made Gracie before she passed away, that he would do everything to help her through this ordeal.

Sophia wanted to tell him about the letter she found today, but something in her heart kept her from doing so. These were so precious to her that Sophia didn't want to risk anyone saying anything negative about these letters, so she kept them all hidden in a beautiful hand-made wooden box that she had received as a gift from her dad when they discovered Grace was sick. He told her that he wanted Sophia to keep all of her special memories in that box so she would never forget them. The box was big enough to keep photo albums, books, and now the beautiful pink envelopes with the precious letters that she was discovering.

As she began getting back into her daily routines, Sophia realized that she would never be the same as she was before her mom's passing but she also knew that she had to continue going to school, eating daily, and somehow manage to gain the motivation to create new goals in her life. With each passing day Sophia learned to embrace the moments of joy she would experience, whether they were in the form of excitement about her new adventure into pageants or her starting to work more with the animal shelter. She had been on the side of depression and despondency and with time her heart was beginning to slowly mend and allow Sophia moments of joy and peace.

These she didn't take for granted because one thing Sophia did realize as she progressed through the moments of grieving, that time does have an amazing ability to help heal the heart but so did the letters she was receiving. The times when she felt happy, she was able to recall memories that only she and her mom shared, and these memories were becoming the catalyst to wanting to make a difference in another's life even if it was walking animals that nobody wanted at the time. Sophia found solace at the animal shelter because when she walked the dogs, she didn't have to worry about carrying on a conversation or holding her attention on another person.

Animals were so happy just to get a small amount of affection and love, and they returned it tenfold to that person who just took moments out of their day to love on them. Through volunteering at the animal shelter, Sophia learned a sense of gratitude that she had never experience before, and the more she learned of stories behind these innocent creatures, the more she wanted to help them. Some of these animals had never experienced the luxury of having a loving home with people surrounding them who valued them. Many were found on streets, rescued from hoarders who just wanted to make money from selling them, or were removed from their homes due to neglect and abuse.

Many ran away and more were left wandering the streets only to be encountered by people who didn't want to take the time or energy to rescue them and help place them in foster or permanent homes. The more immersed Sophia became in her volunteer work, the more she wanted to raise awareness and get the community involved in helping support the shelter and adopt these animals. She began healing as she shared her love to heal some of these animals, whether it was spending an hour a day to help clean the beds and feed the animals or walking or holding them, she was healing more and more as each month passed.

Sophia talked to the managers of the local animal shelters about holding fund raisers for much needed food, blankets, immunizations, and spaying and neutering the animals, Sophia helped in any way that she could and was able to begin getting her friends involved as well. The pageant platform became secondary to her and the goal of getting more and more animals adopted out to good homes became Sophia's primary mission. One by one, volunteers began donating their time, resources, and anything they could to help the community shelter.

Sophia was even able to get coverage through the local media and once a week, they would highlight an animal that was up for adoption. As her dad watched the progression of his daughter, he felt a sense of accomplishment. Not for himself, but for her strength to endure the pain and struggle of watching her mom get sick and the progression of how the cancer took her strength and finally her life. He was so proud of Sophia and knew that somewhere in the perfect world, there was a heaven and Sophia's mom was watching over her and experiencing the same pride that he was at this very moment.

As Sophia continued to work with the animal shelter, she began wanting to spend time with her friends a little bit more and being isolated a little bit less. The comfort she once took from the feeling of isolation was being replaced with the support and solidarity that she was experiencing with her friends. This was part of the healing process and one that her dad was hoping would come soon enough. Life was slowly starting to become easier, and although the struggles of holiday's and moments when mothers were to be celebrated, Sophia struggled through them but had her love of animals to help her through the pain.

One afternoon when Sophia was putting away cleaning supplies, the animal shelter received a telephone call informing them that 37 dogs had just been seized from a hoarder and many of these were in bad condition. They were placing calls to animal shelters within 60 miles to see if they could distribute some of these dogs to each of the shelters so one would not be burdened with almost 40 new animals. As the calls went out, Sophia ran into the office and listened to the conference call. She learned that many of these animals had been abused from the hoarders as well as the other animals in the room with them for so long that they were not sure these dogs could be placed.

Sophia sat in the room as the prepared a plan to take in almost a third of these dogs while placing calls to other shelters in surrounding communities to do the same. Within the hour all 37 dogs had placement in shelters and were on their way to being properly cared and placed in either foster or permanent homes. Sophia gathered blankets, food bowls, and all of the necessary things she would need to ensure the transition of receiving these dogs was as smooth as possible. She called her dad and told him the events that just unfolded and asked permission to stay late at the shelter.

As these animals came into the shelter, Sophia's heart broke because so many had fur that needed to be shaved down due to matting from lack of grooming. They were underweight, some hurt, and all very frightened. Sophia took time with all of the volunteers to nurture the dogs, feed them, and give them one on one attention. There was one dog in particular who caught Sophia's attention as she bent down to pick him up. He was a small Pomeranian who was underweight and terrified of being picked up. Slowly Sophia cared for him every day until he became more comfortable around her and allowed her to carry him.

As she held the dog known as R37 (Red dog who was rescued 37th out of 39 dogs) she sat back on the pillow and just held him close to her. She heard a familiar voice who said, "You're very good with animals lady bug." A startled Sophia looked up to see Albert standing in front of her and in his arms was also a beautiful dog. Before Sophia could speak, Albert continued. "By holding this dog in your arms you are able to see that loss and grief come in many forms. These animals are grieving from a loss of love and trust towards others, and many are now broken spirits who need a lot of love so they can learn to trust again. You are also realizing that there is loss in this world everyday whether it is a loss of a friendship, spouse, job, or a family member. Loss is loss and although the severity is different, the feelings are often the same. Of course, the pain suffered by the loss of a loved one can never be compared to the feelings of a loss of a job, people still suffer in their own way."

Albert didn't move, but continued talking to Sophia, "the most important lesson you can learn through this incident of animal abuse and neglect is that within every soul lies a heart and spirit that can and is often broken. How we learn to heal ourselves and realize that we are all connected to one another is the key that will help you along your journey through life. Ladybug in your arms lays a helpless animal whose heart and spirit became broken from the neglect of another, yet he feels pain nonetheless. You are able to help heal his heart and the heart of many souls when you learn that one small act of kindness can change the life of another. Whether it is the life of a person or an animal, lives are all important to God. "

Sophia stared at Albert and absorbed every word he was saying to her as she held the small dog even closer to her heart as Albert continued. "You just need to understand that all creatures are God's creatures, and the ripple effect of love you spread to even one of these creatures is as important as the love you send out in prayer to many." Albert stopped and smiled at Sophia then pulled a small pink envelope out of his pocket and handed it to her. "Sophia Rose, your mom wants you to know that she is so proud of you."

Sophia looked at the letter in her hand as tears began welling in her eyes. "Albert, how do you know my mom?" she asked as she looked back up at where he was once standing and realized that Albert was gone. Sophia jumped to her feet and with the small dog tucked underneath her arm, she ran into the office where several employees and volunteers were still tending to the animals. Out of breath, Sophia asked if any of them had seen an older gentleman here just moments ago.

"What did he look like," one volunteer asked and Sophia proceeded to describe Albert from the clothes he was wearing, to the cane he kept clutched in his right hand. She described his bow tie and the rosy cheeks he had, especially when he laughed. But most importantly she described him as someone who made her feel as if she were the only person in the world when he was listening to her talk. One of the employees looked suspiciously at the manager then back to Sophia. "We have all seen him Sophia," she said as she stood up and walked to a large framed photo behind the manager's office door. "You are describing Albert, he and his wife started the shelter many years ago."

Sophia stared at the photo and said, "Yes, that's him!" she shouted as she walked towards the photo. "Where is he?" The volunteers turned their attention back to the manager who was staring at Sophia as if she had two heads, "Sophia," she said slowly. "Albert and his wife passed away over 10 years ago. When she died of a sudden heart attack, he stopped coming to visit the shelter and sat on a park bench at their favorite beach every day. It's as if he were waiting for her to come back. One day he got very sick and had to be hospitalized for several months. He died in the hospital."

Sophia felt the blood rush out of her head and thought she was going to pass out. All she could do was nod and walk down the hall, still holding the fragile dog in one arm and the letter in her right hand. She sat down in a quiet corner of the shelter and opened the letter. As she saw her hands shaking, she pulled the dog up to her face and just held him close to her for several moments until she could stop shaking and gather her composure.

Before opening the letter, she knew that this small and frightened dog was meant to be hers and she was going to take him home and adopt him into their family. Sophia kissed the small animal on the head and carefully opened the letter. As she began to read, tears streamed down her face.

My Dearest Sophia,

The Balance of Power

I am beyond amazed at you my precious child. Every day I watch you progress through your journey and grow into your own truth. You have been slowly growing out of your perception of grief and overwhelming sorrow, and coming into a place of love and comfort. Grief can be such an overwhelming emotion, that it paralyzes your spirit and leaves you unable to move out of the sorrow only to be overtaken by it. How you have handled your sadness in my loss is something you should be proud of, because you are learning that your soul possesses the balance of power to heal itself and learn to love again. Someday soon, your father will be able to do the same, but for now he is in a place of sadness not only for his loss of a wife and soul mate, but for your loss of a mother and the other half of you.

Your father is grieving for both of you, and he will heal as he watches you heal in due time. Because he has not been open to my visits in his dreams, he cannot connect with me on the soul level that you have allowed me to connect with you. His fear overtakes his sense of truth, and because he is such a logical man he refuses to allow himself the freedom to believe in things he cannot see….you do. Soon however, your father will allow himself permission to move out of his state of grief and realize that his connection to me does not lie in his sorrow but in his love. That will never cease, it will only grow stronger because I have nothing holding me back anymore in the physical limits.

For now Sophia, I would like you to continue supporting him through his sadness and helping him remember what it feels like to laugh again. His hurt won't allow for the gift of laughter, and he needs that so badly right now. Encourage him to walk on the beach, or go camping, and do things that we used to do. If he refuses, then suggest you both do new things that we never did as a family, so you can create new memories that won't replace me but rather uplift me. His love for you is so deep that he will do nearly anything at this point to see you smile, and he needs to feel needed. Your father is so afraid that he will lose you too Sophia, that his fear is preventing his own life from moving forward.

Do you see now the struggle between the two emotions of love and fear that your father deals with? His internal conflict prevents him from gaining power over his fear so he can move into a perception of love, and slowly learn to enjoy living a happy life again. When he realizes, as you are doing, that he also holds within himself the ability to heal and live life fully again, your father will gain the balance of power of love that fear is holding over him. He will balance experiencing the fear and the sadness of my passing, but he will also create moments of joy and experiences of love in his life once again. Since your father is in such emotional pain, he cannot realize the truth of the power he has to ease his own pain and learn to live beyond it.

I feel that your father is in fear that if he releases his pain of grief, then he in a sense is releasing me. Nothing could be further from the truth of this because my love for him never intended to be replaced by fear. Since I am not there in physical form to remind him of this Sophia, then when you are ready you must be the one to teach him. You don't need to teach him in words but instead teach him with your actions, because he watches you as you remind him so much of me and he doesn't want to forget me.

There is a sense of fear that you too have experienced my precious daughter, and that is the fear of no longer remembering the one you loved when they pass away and cross over. This fear can be so terrifying that those who experience it make themselves believe that the loved one lost remains alive in the pain of the one left behind. Pain is pain and fear is fear, but when grief strikes a soul through the loss of a loved one, they cope the best way they can and often don't have the strength to fight the "illusions" their broken heart is creating. They must be reminded in a gentle manner that the loss of a loved one in the physical sense means they no longer get to see or touch that person, it doesn't mean that the person is no longer in existence.

It becomes hard to battle these false beliefs, and the oftentimes the ones left behind are the souls who need to remember their truth at a soul level. We all come into this journey of life to experience love through one another, and when our lives are complete and we are ready on a soul level to cross over, it doesn't mean that we are any less alive. It just means that you do not see us the way you used to see us when we were in physical form. These letters and dreams you are having of me are my way of communicating with you because you only listen to your heart in your sleep. You cannot be distracted by events or people outside of you while you are sleeping Sophia, so I am able to talk to you and connect with you in a way you will know is true.

I speak to you so many nights and moments in your day, but you struggle to believe that I am here, so it becomes easier to connect with you while you sleep. The next time that your Daddy is sleeping, maybe you can remind him his truth. Speak to him in a gentle manner where you will not wake him, rather remind him that it is ok to heal and remind him that I continue to live through him in our love. Tell him that he needs to grant himself permission to move on and smile in those moments when he wants to smile, but feels guilty because he is not mourning me when he is happy. You are not supposed to mourn for me in sorrow, rather rejoice in my life by living abundantly in yours. Can you do this for me my sweet child? When you are ready....

Meanwhile, know that I am always near you and smiling at your achievements and holding you in my energy while you are sad. Always remember that I am only a thought away.

I love you forever,

Momma

Pageant Preparation
Chapter 16

Every day Sophia prepared for the pageant, and as she worked on volunteering and making a difference through her community service, she grew more and more anxious about the upcoming competition. Sophia loved her new dog and named her "Ladybug" because of the remarkable letters and friendship from Albert. Although she realized that he was in fact someone who had passed on in spirit, she would never forget his words of strength and wisdom and the fact that his appearance was more evidence that these letters she was receiving from her mom may in fact be from the "other side."

Sophia chose not to share with anyone else about Albert because she didn't want to risk appearing like a crazy grieving daughter, and his friendship was entirely too special for her to have to explain to anyone. Whenever Sophia played with Ladybug, she smiled about the memory of Albert and how he appeared and disappeared as quickly as a magician and those memories were gift enough for her. Thinking about winning the state pageant was special for Sophia because her mom loved to watch pageants and always encouraged her to enter only if she ever felt like she wanted to compete against herself.

Always try to become a better version of yourself Sophia, her mom would say. *Whether you compete with yourself in a sport, through your art and writing, or through pageantry, realize that these illusions of competition are in fact created to make you become better than you were the day before.* Sophia remembered her mom's words like it was yesterday and she knew, having learned a mindset of self-sufficiency from her parents that she didn't need to win over anyone else to become a better version of herself. Sophia only needed to take the giant leap of faith and strive to become smarter, healthier, more in gratitude and more comfortable in her own skin.

One afternoon when Sophia was outside playing with Ladybug, her dad walked out into the yard and began throwing the stick to Ladybug who preferred to play tug of war with it rather than chase it and bring it back. He studied Sophia as they watched Ladybug running back to them with the stick in her mouth, then asked Sophia. "Sweetie, do you need any help preparing for your pageant?" She looked puzzled at him as they both began laughing. "I know that I can't teach you how to walk in heels or strut your stuff on the stage," he continued, "but do you need any help with your platform'

Sophia watched ladybug as she ran after the stick her dad threw back out in the yard and thought about it for a moment. "I am having a hard time with my platform Daddy," she replied. "I know that I love animals and want people to adopt homeless animals but..." her voice dropped and she looked down at the green grass she was standing on. "But what?" her dad asked. Sophia looked up at him with a worried expression and said, "I feel my heart is not into it as much as I thought I would be. I feel as if I am missing something and I don't know what that is." Sophia remained quiet for a few more minutes then said, "Daddy, do you think I should be using breast cancer as my platform?"

Sophia's dad's heart jumped for joy as he listened intently to his daughter's voice, but he remained expressionless as he didn't want his desire for her platform to change because of what he wanted for her. "I think you should do whatever your heart is telling you to do Sophia. This journey is about you and how you can make a difference, not only in your own life but in the life of others." He stopped talking for a moment, waiting for Sophia to interject her thoughts but she remained silent so he continued. "Sophia, you have dealt with a lot of sorrow this past year especially, and maybe you can find a way to empower yourself through that sorrow and create joy by helping another person who might be suffering the way you did."

Sophia inhaled deeply and held her breath for several seconds before releasing her breath. She learned to do this technique from Dr. Archer who taught her the importance of releasing stress and anxiety through deep breathing. "Daddy I think I am supposed to talk about helping women find breast cancer early and even help those whose family members are going through it, but don't know if I'm ready. " Sophia looked earnestly at her dad as if she was seeking reassurance from him in some way, and of course he was ready to give it to her.

"Sophia I think that you should identify exactly how you can help another person who may be diagnosed someday with breast cancer, and also look at possibilities as to how you can offer support to those family members and friends who are hurting watching their loved ones fight this disease. Nobody knows it better than you do because you just experienced it, and maybe you can find comfort in comforting another person. Sometimes honey we are called to undergo painful experiences so we can help ourselves become closer to God and help others find their way to Him and to a higher source of greatness. Nobody can explain why your mom had to suffer for so long and ultimately lose her battle to cancer, but if there is something of value that you can gain from the experience, then it helps to empower yourself with that knowledge."

She smiled as the words of her dad were resonating within Sophia's spirit. The more she listened to him talk, the better her heart felt and suddenly she realized that goose bumps were filling her arms and making the hair on her arms and legs stand on end. "You're giving me goose bumps Daddy," she said. " There are so many times that I lie awake at night and ask God why momma...why did she have to get sick and die when so many people who are older than me still have their mom's. I even get mad at God and then I don't want to pray anymore, but as soon as I get mad there is something in my heart that knows I still love him and trust him."

Just then Ladybug ran up to Sophia and licked her face, and while she began trying to crawl up Sophia's chest, both she and her dad began to laugh. "It looks like Ladybug thinks you can do this," Sophia's dad said..."and so do I." Sophia smiled at him and kissed Ladybug and she set her back down on her lap again. "Daddy, what if I don't have the strength to talk about momma without crying? What if the judges think that I am a bumbling idiot in the interview room, and what if I get asked a question on-stage where I begin to cry?"

"Those are all very real concerns honey," her dad replied. "What if you help another young girls mom get diagnosed early and save her life because she had her mammogram, and what if something you say will help a father reach out to his grieving kids when he is so broken he is barely keeping his head above water, and what if," her dad paused and looked down at Sophia. "What if you say or do something that will change the world, one person at a time?" His smile widened as he looked into Sophia's eyes and saw a glimmer of light sparkle from behind them. "Oftentimes Sophia, people are called to do things outside of our comfort zone without fully understanding why. If you pray about it and trust that God will help you through it, then you may surprise yourself as to how the story unfolds."

Sophia studied her dad and reached her arms around his neck and held him tightly. "Daddy, thank you." He smiled back at her and replied, "for what honey?" "Daddy," she said, "thank you for reaching out to me when you were so broken that you were barely keeping your head above water. " Sophia's voice cracked and she fought back the tears as she felt her dad's body shake under her arms while he sobbed. He cried tears of sorrow for losing the love of his life and tears of joy for the blessing of his beautiful wife leaving behind a constant reminder of her love for him.

As they held each other and embraced tightly, Sophia felt a sense of relief and comfort overcome her spirit. It felt as if something had been released that was weighing her heart down for months, and although she couldn't identify what that was, she felt in gratitude that it was gone and she felt lighter again. Sophia knew that she needed to be true to herself and to this journey her family had endured, for this pageant experience to her was not about winning or losing but about how she could take something very painful and make a better version of herself in the process of renewing her spirit.

Later that evening Sophia began completing her pageant application and developing her platform. She smiled as she wrote the words next to her platform cause, *Breast Cancer Awareness - Saving Lives Through Early Detection.* Sophia smiled as she read these words and suddenly the fear she had been experiencing was quickly replaced with joy and excitement. She would use this pageant to honor her mom, her battle with cancer, and celebrate the lives of all the millions of women who had battled this disease. As Sophia closed her computer, she felt a sense of love fill her as if she were being enveloped with a blanket of energy around her small body. Sophia closed her eyes and relished in the feeling of this embrace until it passed.

She knew that this opportunity to enter a pageant and try to heal a broken part of her mom's death would help her to find a way to make a difference in the life of another person. Even if it was one girl who was frightened from a diagnosis of her mom or sister, or a brother who was afraid to cry, Sophia felt in her heart that this was something bigger than herself and this just might be a journey that she may be able to make sense of while she grew into a greater version of herself.

Value vs. Worth
Chapter 17

After weeks of researching breast cancer websites, emailing different chapter representatives, and developing a plan of action, Sophia's head felt as if it were spinning with information yet she felt immobilized in what direction she wanted to proceed. Sophia read countless stories of cancer survivors and she became inspired and depressed, and the staggering statistics of breast cancer survivors vs. those who fought and lost the battle became too much for Sophia to bear.

She began withdrawing once again into her own safe "cocoon" that she had built after her mom's death, and she began to embrace the feelings of sorrow that she had known so well once before. As the days progressed and Sophia's nightmares returned, her dad began having second thoughts as to whether or not she should even be entering a pageant. Maybe it was too soon and she has not had the chance to heal completely or maybe they were both trying to push the healing process forward too quickly.

Sophia's dad wanted more than anything to see his daughter heal from this entire ordeal and the more he wished for Gracie to be alive, the more he became panicked that he was not enough of a parent to guide his daughter beyond the grief. *Oh Gracie*, he thought. *Why did it have to be you to go first? You were the better parent and especially for our daughter. I should have been the one to go first, but instead you once again overestimated me. I don't know what I'm doing here...give me a sign, something that will give me hope and something to hold onto.*

One Sunday afternoon as Sophia was preparing lunch for their weekly picnic, Sophia nonchalantly asked her dad...."Daddy, would you be mad at me if I decided not to enter this pageant?" Sophia's dad stopped putting the cut sandwiches into the baggies and turned to look at his daughter for several seconds then said, "Sophia I will support you in anything you decide to do." He paused and considered his words carefully then said, "Honey, I can't even imagine how you must be feeling right now. All I know is that I have watched you struggle through your mom's illness, watched her suffer, embraced hope when her ultrasounds showed improvement, then ultimately have your spirit crushed when she lost her battle. To watch your journey has made me cry for you, hope for you, and ultimately be inspired by you, and be so proud of you."

Sophia stopped preparing the sandwiches and looked up at her dad, searching his eyes for meaning and just stared at him as she watched him nervously shift from one foot to another. "Anyway, I feel as though I have pressured you into competing in this pageant and trying to get you to do something that you may not be prepared for. You don't have to do this Sophia, there is absolutely nothing you have to prove for anyone...do you understand this?" As her dad stared at Sophia, she fought the urge to run into his arms because she needed to prove that she was in fact ready.

"Daddy," Sophia said. "What if I don't win this pageant? What if all of momma's pain and suffering doesn't make a difference? What if momma died for nothing?" As Sophia heard herself utter these words, she broke down and all of the fears and emotions of insecurities came flooding into her heart and the floodgates broke down and Sophia broke down and cried. "What was I thinking Daddy?" she shouted, and as her anger grew her voice became louder. "Why?" Sophia shouted. "Why, Momma?" There are so many girls who hate their mom's and I loved momma! Why did my mom have to die?"

Sophia's anger rose to a level that not even she had experienced, and as her dad tried to reach out to her to hold her, Sophia pushed away from him and tried to run away and escape his grasp. "Sophia!" he cried out as he caught her thin arms in his hands and pulled her towards him. Grasping at every ounce of courage he had, Sophia's dad pulled her towards him and stared her in the eyes. "There is nothing you have to do to prove to anyone that your mother was an amazing woman. There is not one single soul who has to be convinced that she made a difference in this world other than the souls she touched. Most importantly, there is not one person who needs to be convinced that you loved her with all of your heart other than yourself."

As these words resonated throughout Sophia's entire body, she stared at her dad as he showed a new side of himself that Sophia had never seen. He showed a vulnerable side, a courageous side, but most importantly, he revealed a side that was real and fragile. Sophia fell to her knees sobbing as her dad pulled her up into his arms and gently lifted her up into his lap.

He remained silent as she wept for her pain, for the loss of her mom, and for the realization that there was absolutely nothing anyone could do to bring her mom back to her.

Every night someone would have their mom tuck them into bed, and every day there would be countless girls who would be sassing off to their mom's, disrespecting them, arguing with them, and wishing they were no longer in their lives. Every day there would be thousands of girls wishing that their mothers were non-existent in their lives, and she was one of the many who would have given her left arm to have just one more moment with her mom. How she could ever convey this message seemed hopeless to Sophia and the more she thought about it, the more upset she became.

Sophia reminisced about the memories she had of her mom and if she could hold just one recollection in her heart, Sophia would have held the memory of what it felt like to have her mom hold her just one more time. The more she held the memories, the more upset she became until Sophia finally allowed the tears to flow that she had been fighting for the past several weeks. "Daddy," she cried. "I have tried not to cry for so many weeks, but I am so mad!" Sophia searched her dad for anything that would enlighten her.

"Sophia, my beautiful baby girl…there is nothing I can say to you that will ever release you of this pain. You will reach out to the survivors who fought this battle and won, and you will reach out to those who lost loved ones. It is crucial to remember that each person who fought this battle is just as heroic as the soul who lost the fight. There are winners in the fight against cancer and there are perceived losers, but we don't know the journey that those who lost their battle had. Maybe your mom wanted you to continue to raise awareness about early detection so more people will beat this disease."

"By honoring the spirit of the people who both won and lost the battle, you allow yourself the opportunity to have a voice where you were not allowed one before. When your mom was sick, you prayed to God for her healing but you watched helplessly as she slowly lost her grip on life. Sophia your voice was heard although you felt that it wasn't, because God hears and feels every prayer from you. Even though you wanted your mom to be healed, you don't know the journey that she was on before she even came to this world." Sophia looked puzzled yet listened intently to her dad as he continued. "Sweetheart, we will never know why mom was afflicted with cancer let alone why she had to die from it. What we do know is what you can do with the legacy you leave behind for her."

As Sophia examined her dad's face, she realized that there was a great deal of truth behind his words. She had not considered that although she couldn't help her mom beat cancer, she would do something to help other people learn about their own bodies and how they can practice early detection. Maybe one day she can help save another young girl's mom from being diagnosed too late, and through her platform she might be able to even save another person's life. Sophia took a deep breath and thought for a moment then said, "Daddy, what if I can't talk about it? What if I can't talk about momma getting sick...I don't think I can."

Her dad pulled her towards him and lifted Sophia's chin so her eyes would meet his. "Sophia, I will help you learn what parts of your mom's journey you are comfortable talking about and what parts we need you to keep private. Your mom was a story teller and she taught you about sharing parts of life without losing composure, so we will figure out how you can share your story of mom without crossing the threshold and losing your composure in front of the judges." Sophia smiled and agreed because she finally began feeling empowered by this pageant and felt there was something deep within her heart that was pushing her towards this.

Taking the first step of faith by entering the pageant, then following that with a huge leap of faith and exploring what she wanted to share and how she was going to share her story made Sophia feel as if she may actually be able to accomplish this goal. It felt good that Sophia was finally focusing on something other than being sad, and she knew this would be good for her. Accepting her dad's help in the process would help them grow closer and become advocates together. Although Sophia knew that she wanted to enter this pageant, there was still a part of her that lacked the confidence of being able to make a difference.

What if people didn't want to hear her story and what if nobody listened to her because she was young? Although her mom fought cancer she still lost her battle and what if people didn't respect her journey? All of these fears began to rush through Sophia's head and the more she thought about them, the more anxious she became. *Momma, how am I going to do this for us? I wish I could use your ability to tell a story to make people listen. What if I'm not smart enough, pretty enough, or good enough to win this pageant? What am I doing?* As Sophia leaned back against her chair, she closed her eyes and began thinking of the various ways that this goal could quickly derail and turn into an ugly train wreck.

Just then Ladybug ran into the room and jumped up on Sophia's lap and began licking her face. Sophia opened her eyes and sat up abruptly as she pulled her face away from Ladybugs frantic tongue. "Ladybug, you scared me," Sophia laughed as she looked down to pet the dog that was still wagging her tail and trying to turn Sophia's face into a lollypop. She lifted the dog into her arms and walked her over to Ladybug's pillow so she could lay her down for a nap. Still full of energy, the dog had no interest in sleeping as she wanted to play with Sophia so instead of putting her down again, Sophia decided to lie down on the bed with Ladybug so she could help her fall asleep.

As Sophia closed her eyes, the aroma of roses filled the air and as Sophia noticed the scent her skin grew cold. It felt as if the air conditioner had been turn down to freezing and even Ladybug sat up and looked around the room. As Sophia sat up and looked around she realized there was a pink envelope lying on the bed next to Ladybug! Sophia grabbed the envelope and ran outside of the room, just to see if her dad had walked out or was anywhere near her bedroom. As Sophia searched up and down the hallway, she didn't see any trace of her dad or anyone else for that matter.

Holding the envelope in one hand, Sophia closed the door behind her with the other and sat down on the bed pulling Ladybug closer to her. She opened the pink envelope and began to read….

My Dearest Sophia,

Value vs. Worth

There is an abundant illusion that has been taught from generation to generation for far too long. That is the illusion between value and worth, which has been misleading millions of souls into believing they are not valuable. Where do you define value and worth and how do you apply it to your journey through this experience in life? From childhood, we are taught from our parents that our worth is equated to the value that another soul wants to place upon it. Very rarely are children taught that their value and self-worth are to be defined by their own measure rather than that of another. If you spend your entire life trying to be defined as valuable by another, then you will rarely find that which you are seeking.

Why? Because you cannot ask another soul who is also searching for their own value and worth to define yours or else you will end up setting your own measurements on their set of standards rather than your own. Remember when you submitted your art piece for the local Art Contest in school, and although you worked very hard to perfect your skills, you were not selected as the contest winner. Since you had placed so much time and energy on designing your beautiful art, a piece of your soul was imprinted through your energy onto the canvas. When the judges overlooked your work, you took the pain of not being validated by another to heart, and decided that you were not a good enough artist to continue painting. Rather than find another contest to enter, you placed your brushes in a drawer along with your own self-worth and have yet to pick up your paint brush and do what you enjoy – create art as a healthy form of self-expression.

How did another person's opinion of your artwork become more valuable to you than your own opinion of your talent? Yet you did what too many souls do when they are not validated by another soul, you think yourself less worthy or less talented and cease to continue perfecting your craft. Why didn't you stop to consider that the soul who was judging your artwork was not a representation of the truest and most perfect artist in the world? Although this judge was selected by another to judge a contest, what made that person's opinion of your talents more valuable to you than your own opinion of your work? Did you ever stop to consider that maybe the process you went through during the competition was to teach you that you are the most important judge of your work?

How many souls walk this journey through life with their canvas and brushes tucked away in a dark drawer because one or several other souls failed to validate their worth? Too many people have hidden their potential and robbed themselves of knowing their true worth, because they have learned to place the value of their own skills and talents in the hands of another person's opinion. This is one of the greatest illusions that we on the other side watch our loved ones experience, and too many of us who have crossed over are comforting those precious souls while they sleep. We want so badly for each of you to equate your value to who you are rather than what you do. The value of a soul who works tirelessly picking up bins of trash everyday so you can enjoy a clutter-free and sanitary home is just as high as the soul who is a successful business owner and has their own personal plane for travel. That business owner needs the services of the person who works at the waste management service and he is no less valuable because he makes less money than the business owner.

What has happened is that so many souls in this journey through life equate their value based on what society dictates as their worth. The two are completely separate because God *created us from a piece of His soul, and we are no less valuable than God. How then do we dare to compare our value and worth to what society, our friends, neighbors, or family deem to be our worth? Sophia, the most valuable piece of advice I can give you is this... you are valuable beyond measure. Never allow society or anyone else to convince you that your worth equates to the amount of money that you make. Your value is about who you are not what you do. There is no measure to the human spirit, so how can you allow others to convince you that your value is based upon how much money you make.*

Sophia, find your passion and dedicate your life to pursuing it. You are a co-creator with God and your energy is not meant to remain stagnant in a job that you dislike or a relationship that you are not fulfilled with. This includes a relationship at any level my child, whether it is your dearest friend or your longtime boyfriend. Your energy seeks to grow and reinvent itself through your experiences, so never fall prey to old patterns and living your life in auto-pilot. The moment you choose to do turn your thinking off and turn on the auto pilot is the moment when you will continue repeating the same actions and thus experience the same results. You will become trapped in your own life and risk becoming comfortable in this pattern whether it is for your greater good or not.

Learn to be proactive in your own life, and realize your own worth. Never allow another to become a substitute for your power. You have a voice and that voice must be heard by yourself first and foremost. Always equate your value to the fact that you are a child of God and you are valuable whether another person validates you or not. This is not only an important lesson in the world but especially in the world of pageantry when you are being judged by others who may not have even accomplished a fraction of what you have. Keep your perspective in order and you will never have to remind yourself that you are worthy of accomplishing your greatest aspirations.

I am so proud of you my precious child and will always love you. Remember that I am just a thought away.

I love you forever,

Momma

Beauty Lies Within
Chapter 18

As the weeks progressed, Sophia became immersed in her pageant preparation and began filling the guest room with dresses, shoes, jewelry, and other pageant essentials. Her dad spent hours with Sophia working on developing her plan of action for her platform and helped Sophia understand where she became very uncomfortable talking about her mom's illness. The more she worked on sharing the story with relevant information, the easier it became to transition into her statistics about breast cancer facts, and ultimately what she wanted to accomplish with her goal if she were to win the pageant.

Sophia researched information on the internet and discovered pageant books to help her develop her interview skills. . From these books, Sophia learned how to develop her platform and learned how to articulate her thoughts in the judge's interview room. Sophia even talked her dad into hiring a personal pageant coach so she could learn interview techniques, and how to walk on-stage with confidence. She even learned how to develop her image and brand herself as a competitor as well as learned how to select her wardrobe and apply make-up. Sophia was so happy that this pageant coach was able to help her with her entire pageant preparation, but nobody was more relieved than her dad.

As he watched his daughter transform herself from a sad young girl to an empowered and confident young woman, relief filled his heart. He would have done anything to help Sophia go through the grieving process, and now he could do something to help her learn to smile again from the inside out. As Sophia gained confidence through working with Miss Ariel, her pageant coach, she learned to discover that she can become empowered once again by speaking her voice and sharing staggering statistics about breast cancer that would make people want to get involved. Whether it was to raise money for research or spread the word about early detection, Sophia was gaining strength through advocacy and focusing her attention to growing into a better version of herself.

The months progressed and Sophia worked hard on her fitness so she could have great muscle definition for her swimsuit competition. Sophia also started wearing makeup to school every day so she could practice applying it, as well as learning how to style her long hair. The local newspaper even ran a small article on her with her photo revealing that she would be competing in the state pageant in a few weeks which drew unwanted attention to Sophia. She noticed a group of girls standing outside of the school and as she walked past them, Sophia overheard one of the girls comparing her to the other photos of the contestants which had been put up on the internet pageant website.

"She's not as pretty as some of the other ones," Sophia heard one popular girl say. "I mean she's cute but she's not beautiful. If I were her, I would be terrified that I wasn't pretty enough." As the other girls giggled, Sophia looked at the group and noticed one of the girls in that group was also a contestant in the state pageant. Sophia told herself not to pay attention to them because they were just trying to intimidate her, but their words cut through her self-esteem like a knife.

As Sophia stood in front of the mirror and washed her face that night, she stared at herself and the words that she overheard the group of girls say were playing over and over again in her mind. What if she wasn't pretty enough to compete in this pageant? As much as she didn't want to admit it, now that Sophia was feeling good about her platform she realized just how badly she wanted to win this pageant. If the judges didn't think she was pretty enough to win, then all of her work was going to be limited and Sophia wanted so much to take her platform to a national level so she could make a difference on a larger level.

Pulling up the contestant photos on the internet became Sophia's main focus and rather than spending her time developing her skills in preparation for the pageant, Sophia became obsessed with studying the other contestants and comparing herself to those she would be competing with. Suddenly Sophia's shift of focus switched from feeling good about herself, and the accomplishments she had made in the past several months to what the other contestants were doing and how they looked.

Sophia's pageant coach even noticed a difference in her self-confidence and realized that she was feeling more insecure about herself and her appearance. When asked about the change in Sophia, she merely responded by saying it was pageant jitters, but her coach knew better. As they were reviewing Sophia's paperwork and practicing her judge's interview questions, Miss Ariel asked Sophia how she was spending her time preparing for the pageant. Sophia squirmed in her chair and innocently replied, "I am looking at the contestants photos a lot and researching each of them on the internet so she could see who she was competing against.

It was no wonder that Sophia's confidence level had declined and when she was asked why she had been spending so much time looking at other contestants instead of focusing that time on developing her own skills Sophia paused. She looked at Miss Ariel and considered whether or not she should tell her about the comment the girls made at school. As Sophia shared with her pageant coach the details of that encounter, all of her insecurities became very evident to them both. "I don't think I'm pretty enough to win this pageant," Sophia said with a sad tone in her voice. "I would withdraw from the pageant today if it wasn't for the fact that Daddy has invested so much time and money on my pageant preparation."

Miss Ariel listened to Sophia and after she let her share all of her thoughts, Miss Ariel asked, "Sophia, what is your definition of beauty? The question took Sophia by surprise and as she remembered her pageant coaching with the many questions they had practiced, Sophia began to answer but was interrupted. "Tell me from your heart Sophia," Miss Ariel said as she leaned back against her chair and stared thoughtfully at Sophia. "There is no right or wrong answer; I would just like you to share your definition of beauty from your own heart." Sophia took a moment to think and shook her head. "I would have said that beauty is as beauty does but that isn't really answering the question. I think a beautiful person is someone who wants to be of service and shares her compassion and her love with others. I think beauty is also someone who takes care of themselves and takes pride in her appearance."

As Sophia explained her own definition of beauty she heard herself describe all of the traits that her mom had. When she was done explaining, she looked back at Miss Ariel and waited for her to respond. "Sophia, do you believe that you fit your own ideal of beauty?" Miss Ariel asked. As Sophia contemplated her question she began to nod in agreement. "Yes, I do." Sophia replied. Miss Ariel continued, "Nowhere in your definition of beauty did you specifically describe physical traits that a beautiful woman should possess...why?"

Sophia thought about it and answered, "Because I think that everyone is beautiful in their own way. Beauty doesn't come in one hair or eye color, and I have seen beautiful women who are tall and short, as well as all ethnic backgrounds. I don't think there is only one definition of beauty in the physical sense." Sophia replied. Miss Ariel smiled at her and then asked Sophia, "If you believe this then why would you look at the mirror and not think that you are pretty enough?" Sophia smiled awkwardly at Miss Ariel and remained silent and she continued to listen. "Sophia, I think a beauty pageant is a perfect opportunity for women across the world to redefine beauty not to fit into a certain mold of it wouldn't you?

As Sophia shared her fears and concerns about the pageant and the beauty aspect of it, she began feeling better but somewhere inside of her insecurity she could not completely ignore the girls who said that Sophia was not pretty enough to win. Sophia knew that this would be a challenge to overcome and had to work diligently on overcoming this so she didn't feel miserable on the stage. As the pageant session came to an end, Miss Ariel stood up and excused herself for a moment. After a few minutes, she walked back into the room and handed Sophia a small writing journal filled with blank pages. "Sophia," Miss Ariel said. "I want you to write in this journal what your definition of beauty is. Use the world around you and pay close attention to what scenes in your life you consider beautiful and what people specifically in your life exemplify the epitome of beauty." Sophia listened intently to the instructions Miss Ariel was giving her as Miss Ariel continued. "I think it's important for you to know what your definition of beauty is and how it applies to your life and how different forms of beauty make you feel. I think it will surprise you. "Sophia tucked the journal into her tote and hugged Miss Ariel as she rushed out the door to meet her dad who was waiting for her in the car. Out of all of the homework assignments Miss Ariel gave her, Sophia thought this was by far the strangest one yet. After all, what difference did it make to her what she considered beautiful, since the group of judges were going to be the ones to decide.

Later that evening Sophia began making a list of attributes that she considered beautiful in others, just as Miss Ariel had asked her to do. The more Sophia added to her list, the more uncomfortable she became. As she was writing down words such as perfect body, long hair, blue eyes, Sophia realized that nothing on her list remotely described her! As a matter of fact, Sophia was describing her friend Crystal. In Sophia's eyes, nobody could compare to Crystal because she was popular, beautiful, and everybody loved her. . "Ugh," Sophia murmured to herself, "I'm done for." She tossed the journal off to the side of the bed while leaning back and throwing her hands over her face. What in the world was she thinking to remotely consider entering a beauty pageant. After all Sophia considered herself very ordinary, yet even though strangers would complement her often Sophia thought they were just being nice to her. Exhausted and worried, Sophia closed her eyes and began drifting off to sleep. As her thoughts wandered off to considering ways of pulling out of the pageant, she took a deep breath and slowly sighed. As she began falling asleep Sophia heard the sound of a faint whisper.

"Sophia?" Startled, Sophia sat upright and searched the room. Hearing only the sound of her startled breathing, Sophia lunged off the bed and stood next to the door with her hand on the doorknob just in case she had to run out of the room. *Was I dreaming this?* She thought as she caught her breath and sat back down on a chair next to her bedroom door. As Sophia looked around her bedroom, she noticed the journal she had been writing in was sitting neatly on her desk. Puzzled, she remembered having tossed it aside before she closed her eyes, so how did this journal get placed on her desk?

As Sophia picked up the journal, she opened the pages ad read through some of the definitions of beauty she had written down just moments before. Turning the page to continue writing in her journal, Sophia turned pale and her hands began to tremble. As she rifled through the remaining pages of her new journal, she realized were pages and pages of writing in what appeared to be her mother's handwriting!

Sophia turned on the lamp and slowly began reading the words that so graciously filled the pages.

My Dearest Sophia,

Beauty lies within its own perfection

Beauty is undeniable. Everywhere you look there are visions of beauty that often go overlooked or overhyped. What is so amazing to me is the fact that on the other side, everyone radiates such light and an aura of true beauty. I only wish each and every soul could recognize that their own beauty. There are souls who become magnified in your life journey through the television, movies, and even pageants who have undeniable beauty but there are many more souls with the same beauty who are not even looked twice at. How is that?

As you have learned, we are all energetic souls and have the power to magnify and create. What you focus your energy on grows, and what you choose to ignore becomes insignificant in your journey through life. Take for instance some of the beautiful celebrities that you see every day being magnified by the media. Their beauty is just as present as is yours, but because you choose to focus your energy on those figures and consider them the epitome of beauty, you choose to make your own beauty and presence insignificant by ignoring it. Out of choice through your own free will, you make yourself insignificant in your own eyes.

The more you focus your energy on glorifying the beauty of other souls, the less you feed energy to your own soul and allow yourself to realize your own true beauty. There is something very beautiful about each and every soul that walks this journey through life, and if they would each take the time to appreciate the beauty that God has blessed them with, the more confident they would feel and the more enjoyable their journey would be through this experience.

Instead, so many souls focus their attention on growing the energy of those who are portrayed in magazines, television, billboards, and wearing crowns that they don't realize their own worth. How is it that we enter this journey of life to experience it for ourselves, and become transformed into believing an illusion that our life becomes about those around us? If I could have several moments to re-live in my life Sophia, I would have appreciated myself more and focused on those around me less. I would have acknowledged my olive skin rather than comparing it to the beautiful women around me that I deemed more beautiful, and I certainly would have paid more attention to myself.

Rather than looking through magazines at retouched photos of already beautiful models, I would have looked into the mirror to appreciate my eyes and my high cheekbones. Rather than glorifying those around me by giving away my energy to them, I would have gone within myself to acknowledge and feel the blessing of that which I am. That way my own energy would have grown into more confidence and appreciation for myself rather than being hard on myself because I didn't fit into the mold of what society labeled as beautiful. Remember my child that I was the "society" that focused my attention on growing the confidence of those around me through my thoughts, emotions, and actions.

When you begin pursuing pageantry and really understanding that it is about you becoming a better version of yourself, then you will know what it is to be a successful competitor. Allow yourself the permission to glorify yourself through acknowledging your own inner and physical beauty. Grow more confident through feeding yourself the energy that you waste daily on illusions, and spend time and focus your attention to becoming the best version of yourself that you can be at the time you are given. There is no real definition of perfection, because it only exists as you define it.

If you define the perfection of beauty being a tall and elegant brunette, yet you are a petite blonde then you must change your definition of beauty to include petite blondes. If you choose to spend your life comparing yourself against others, then you will always fall short in your own eyes. This is truth because when you compare yourself to another person, then you are automatically searching for faults in either yourself or the person you are comparing yourself to. When you appreciate your own beauty and that of another, then there is no room to find fault because you are consciously acknowledging the perfection of each of you.

I have spent years studying pageantry and the best advice I can give you Sophia is to spend every moment that you wish to compare yourself to another, on developing and acknowledging your own attributes. If women entered the sport of pageantry through the eyes of truth rather than the eyes of fear, just imagine how powerful this experience would be. Rather than trying to look like the outgoing queen, or another person who they deem more beautiful than themselves, contestants need to develop those areas of themselves where they perceive themselves to not be enough. This way, the act of focusing your attention to acknowledging your own beauty and truth will in fact grow your appreciation to yourself.

Enter the world of pageantry from the spirit of truth where you are striving to become a greater version of yourself mind, body, and soul. Reach within those walls of your soul where insecurity and illusion have overtaken confidence and truth. Develop your mind skills to communicate with the world around you and come from that place of contribution where you focus on giving to another something that will make them a greater version of themselves. Spend time practicing a healthy lifestyle, a healthy mind, and a giving heart and you will know what the true meaning of pageantry is. If every woman spent her time creating love in her reality rather than fear in the world of illusions, then every contestant would walk away from a pageant feeling like she has gained exactly what she entered the pageant for. A sense of self, feeling comfortable and happy to be in her own skin, and driven to share her gifts with the world around her.

Remember this when you compete in any pageant, and realize that what you seek to fulfill by entering a pageant lies within you alone. You never need the approval or acceptance of another person to reach your greatest potential, and this lesson is often learned through pageantry. Although it appears from the outside looking in, that these beautiful young women are vying for the approval from a group of five strangers, they are in essence competing against themselves to become a greater version of who they were the day before. They have to fight anxiety, stress, fear, and still be able to communicate effectively. If women learned to step outside of themselves each and every day to become better versions of themselves, and then just imagine how many more dreamers would be successful.

Beauty pageants are businesses, and just like any other businesses they must learn to make a profit in order to be successful. Knowing that they are run through the necessity of profit and loss just as any other business, then how is it that so many young hopefuls place their entire self-worth on the line if this business fails to acknowledge them as the overall winner? Realize my Sophia that you must first learn how to develop your own skills and self-confidence so you need not the approval from strangers to tell you whether or not you are enough.

Learn to become the best version of yourself and embrace your own uniqueness, and the world will follow suit. Beauty lies in its own perfection of confidence and individuality, because within and outside of every individual is a beauty that no other has. What often happens though is that these individuals attempt to become a generic version of everyone else, and suddenly individual beauty is no longer celebrated, but replaced. The perfection of your beauty lies within your different skin color, eye color, hair color, and traits that you have all your own. If everyone walked this journey through life looking like everyone else, then beauty would no longer be celebrated or recognized.

Remain true to yourself and learn how to develop your own God-given talents and beauty to the highest level. Never try to become an imitation of another, or you will slowly convince yourself that you alone are not enough. There are enough voices in the world around you echoing their own insecurity into another's ears. Choose to be the voice of truth that realizes we all possess a trait and a perfection that celebrates God. It would be as if the arms on your body wanted to look like your legs because they are focused on what the legs do rather than what glory they can bring when holding a puppy or another's hand. Each of you plays a role in the completeness of the whole, and without each of your individual parts being different, then God would not get to experience the whole of himself through your journey.

Let the legs experience being legs, the arms experience their greatness, and each part of the whole body of Christ consciousness will be expressed individually. As Sophia, you play your role in the experience of the whole by celebrating your own beauty and recognizing your own worth. No one piece of the union of Source energy is better than another, they only serve to celebrate their own roles in the completion of the whole. This is why comparing yourself to another is a complete waste of time and energy, because each of you has a perfection that lies within your own beauty. Celebrate that perfection and you will enjoy your life to the fullest.

I love you forever,

Momma

Preparing to Win
Chapter 19

With only two weeks left before the state pageant competition, Sophia was feeling confident and prepared. She had connected with a statewide organization that supported breast cancer research and raised awareness to help educate women on the importance of early detection. Sophia had the opportunity to volunteer with this organization and learn how she can help through her own efforts and how she could get others involved as well. The more Sophia learned about this organization and heard stories from cancer survivors, the more she wanted to immerse herself into her platform. Instead of feeling sad by hearing other stories of families who lost loved ones, Sophia became encouraged and inspired by their faith and strength. No longer did she feel alone in the process, but instead she gained strength from those around her who had undergone the same experience.

By now Sophia's pageant walk was effortless, as she practiced walking in her high heels every night while she was preparing dinner and washing the dinner. Just as her pageant coach suggested, Sophia wore her socks with her new heels to break them in so she wouldn't get blisters the week of the pageant. Her swimsuit fit her perfectly and the beautiful evening gown her dad purchased as a surprise gift to her was already altered to fit her like a glove. She was in the process of categorizing her jewelry and accessories to match her pageant wardrobe and tucking them carefully away so they wouldn't break during her trip.

With each passing day Sophia checked items off of her pageant packing list as well as her 'To Do" list that Miss Ariel provided her during one of her pageant coaching lessons. Sophia had become a pro at styling her own hair and creating her makeup to look natural for the judge's interview and more enhanced for the stage lights. As the pageant neared Sophia grew more excited and elated to share her platform with the pageant judges. Somewhere in the process of preparing for her pageant, Sophia found healing through changing her perspective from losing her mom to cancer to being an advocate for others.

Sophia still had pains of sorrow and there were many moments during her preparation that she would cry or become sad from missing her mom. This pageant was something that Sophia and her mom would have loved preparing for together, but through the letters she was receiving and her dad's interest in helping her, Sophia was having many more good days that replaced the bad ones. One afternoon during a long afternoon of school and pageant lessons, Sophia decided to spend some time just reading up on the Law of Attraction at her local bookstore.

Although Sophia's generation was immersed in the social media and internet, Sophia was one of those rare young people who still loved to touch the pages of books and write notes in her binder. She loved the feeling of ear marking book pages and using a bright yellow highlighter to highlight the important sentences or words that struck a chord within her. With the turning of each and every page, Sophia grew more connected to understanding how people can create their life through what they focus their attention on. Her parents had been avid believers in the law of attraction and used it to create successful businesses and her mom used it to transform her career as a teacher to an author.

Sophia always gained inspiration from books and what better place to get some last minute reading in, along well as her caffeine fix than at the local bookstore. After ordering a latte and a muffin, Sophia relished her snack and observed the other people in the bookstore. She knew what section she would be visiting as soon as she ate, because she loved the spiritual and new age section of the bookstore. With her parents teaching her the law of attraction and focusing your energy to create the life and experiences you want, Sophia understood the importance of learning as much about positive thinking; especially now that she was only weeks away from competing in the state pageant.

Taking her time Sophia studied the books on the bookstore shelf and pulled out to read several pages of those books that stressed the importance of positive thinking. She understood the concept but was willing to learn from the experts, so with each book that interested her Sophia riffled through some of the pages on some, and read a chapter or two on others. Every book has a story and although the concept is the same the manner in which it was delivered varied from author to author. Sophia never got bored reading these books because she lived her life in a positive state of gratitude...that is until her mom passed away.

As Sophia touched the books on the bookstore shelf with her index finger, she slowly walked and read the titles of many amazing authors who were familiar to her. Suddenly Sophia stopped in her tracks as her finger touched a book with the name Grace Bello on the stem of the book written in bold white font. Sophia pulled the book out of the shelf and smiled as she looked at the book her mom had written and published several years before she passed away. Even though Sophia had a collection of her mom's books, she stared at this one as if it were brand new and never before seen. As Sophia sat down on the available chair next to the shelves where she discovered the book, Sophia opened the book and began looking through the pages.

She had always been impressed with her mom's writing, and today Sophia looked at the pages of this book as if she were reading her mom's words for the very first time. Sophia searched the chapters and smiled as she read words that she had heard her mom tell her every day of her life, but it seemed different with them written down on the pages of this book. A sense of pride filled Sophia's heart as she carefully turned the pages and swept her hand over the words, as if she were trying to regain a part of her mom that created these chapters.

While Sophia lost herself in the words of her mom's book, she had not realized that she has spent the last two hours at the bookstore. She knew that her dad would be coming home soon and getting worried, so she texted him her whereabouts and informed him she was coming home now. Just as Sophia stood up to place the book back on the shelf, something fell out of between the pages. Sophia's heart skipped a beat when she saw lying on the carpeted floor next to her foot was a small pink envelope with the words *Sophia Rose* written on the front.

Sophia bent down to pick up the envelope and looked around to see if anyone else was watching her, and as she sat back down on the chair Sophia opened the envelope and began reading the letter.

My Dearest Sophia,

Preparing to Win

Winning in pageantry is similar to winning in the game of life — first by realizing that the competition is being played by you alone, and everyone else is playing their own game in their own reality. You are not competing against one another for a coveted prize rather you are walking alongside one another in your journey and encouraging each other to reach their ultimate destination. By understanding what the definition of winning is in your journey, you will know how to recognize it when you attain that final goal. So many people walk along their journey lost without a single clue as to what it is they are striving for, all along trying to take from their neighbor, family, or friend what they have worked for because they feel it is owed to them. Yet they fail to ask themselves what it is that this prize means to them, because what is valuable to one does not necessarily equate to the same value to another.

So many people spend their lives trying to reach one another's goals and never stop to ask themselves why. By knowing what your specific goal is and why it is valuable it is to you, then you know why you are working towards attaining it. That is the number one reason that so many people feel like failures in their lives. They have not established the definition of winning in their journey of life. Winning is not about one giant leap towards a goal, rather it is about tiny steps towards improving one's self during the culmination of their lifetime. When you define winning throughout your moments in life, then you are reaching goals that will move mountains. It can be a goal of getting into physical shape, earning good grades in school, or reaching a specific level of management in your career, but whatever you do you must set the definition of a goal and know when to celebrate your win in achieving it.

Take your journey step by step just as you do when preparing for a pageant and be honest with yourself on the weaknesses you need to refine, and the strengths you need to continue perfecting. This way you walk through your life continually trying to be better than you were before and always being deliberate in your goal so you know what you are working towards. In order to be as deliberate in creating yourself as the Queen you want to become, then you need to peel back the layers that you have built your life from and understand why you think the way you do and what your beliefs are. This way you can identify your strengths as well as your weaknesses. Your layers are delicate just like an onion layer, but they hold your thoughts and emotions, which ultimately create your actions.

Taking time to uncover and identify who you are underneath the beautiful smile, the fit body, and the stylish clothes will keep you grounded and real. Knowledge of the world around you is important in order to understand your surroundings and how you fit into them, but knowledge of the world within yourself is crucial so you know what makes you feel and create love in all aspects of your life. Look at your life like a beautifully constructed house where you live, and the exterior represents your body, clothing, and everything that Is visible to the world. The foundation, walls, and furniture within the house hold the essence of your life and where your sanctuary lies. If the exterior *of the house is presented beautifully to the world, but the walls and foundation are cracking inside, then the house will eventually crumble and fall.*

If you take the time to fix the cracks in the foundation so your house can stand tall and beautiful, you will realize that it is worth the effort in the long run. The walls that create the rooms within the house must also be built for a reason, is to house the different areas that make the house unique and special it its features. These walls are sometimes built because one wants to shut out a dark corner and store things that no longer serve their greater good, and these walls need to come down one by one. As they come down, you can replace them with new walls that allow the doors to open into the adjacent rooms that store the wonderful gifts that create love in your home. Look at your life and how you can improve the construction of your temple, and you will always seek to improve yourself in ways that will bring more love and light into your house.

Pageantry allows you as the contestant to look within the rooms of your life and see which ones you want to share and use the stories hidden within the walls to help another who may be dealing with the same set of circumstances. Whether you help another young girl who is suffering from low self-esteem, or raise money for a charity in your community, pageants open the doors for young women to have a voice and learn to develop themselves. Sophia, when the time is right and you have healed the open wounds created from my passing, you will also assist people who have lost a loved one. Your words will resonate within the walls of their soul and aide in their healing process. Not until you are ready and your spirit is called do you have to even consider this. I know that just the thought of my sickness and the pain caused from my physical death is too much to bear let alone discuss it among a group of strangers. But in time you will find the courage to surrender your faith and walk among those millions who have suffered the same type of pain as you.

Your goal is to write a journal as to how to take your life step by step out of the pain of your soul and move forward one foot at a time. You must make a deliberate decision to reinvent yourself and build your foundation from love rather than fear. My illness caused you so much anxiety that you are afraid of rebuilding your temple in fear that someone else will break the walls down from another devastating pain. Sophia, you must learn how to love again and this process begins with loving yourself. Once you decide to move forward in the process of stepping out of fear, then you begin to feel in control of your life again and this is where the magic happens. My beautiful child, God knows how much you have suffered from my passing and where there Is pain, there is also room for hope. Where there is hope, there is peace and where there is peace there is God. Find God within you in the darkest corners of your walls where you have hidden Him from sight, and allow His presence to bring you back to love.

I am so proud of you my beautiful child, and am thankful that you have acknowledged me in your life. You are the daughter I have waited my whole life for and I am forever proud of the person you are and the young woman you are becoming.

I am so proud of you my precious child and will always love you. Remember that I am just a thought away.

I love you forever,

Momma

Avoid the Blame Game
Chapter 20

The challenges Sophia had faced during her mother's cancer and ultimately her passing were without question the most difficult experiences she had endured. As she prepared for her judges interview, Sophia knew she would have to decide how she was going to share her story without crying and by being as authentic as possible. Sophia had heard rumors of several pageant contestants crying in the judge's interview room during prior competitions and she knew that would not be her legacy in the pageant industry. Even though Sophia and her dad had been preparing for questions that judges could ask in the interview, a small part of her was still anxious that she would not be able to take control of this interview and keep from crying.

Just as she had been instructed by her pageant coach, Sophia developed her mom's story where she could be informative, connect with the judges, and not cry in the process. One afternoon during her pageant lesson, Sophia asked Miss Ariel to explain once more how she can share her information without breaking down in the interview room, and as Sophia pulled out her paper Miss Ariel smiled at her and said. "Sophia, I would like you to set your paper and pen down and just listen to my words." As Sophia put these things down on the table in front of her, Sophia looked back at Miss Ariel and shifted uncomfortably in her chair.

Anytime that she was about to be taken out of her comfort zone, Sophia would get a sense of discomfort in her gut and squirm which would in turn cause Miss Ariel to take notice and say, "Sophia you know that it is my job to get you comfortable being *uncomfortable*. As creatures of habit we create our thoughts, emotions, and actions through repetition and before your realize it, you are an older version of yourself having the same experiences in your life without allowing yourself room to grow into a *greater* version of yourself. My job as your pageant coach is to take you out of your comfort zone so you can continue to grow into a better version of yourself. If I keep you in the same place you were last month or last week, then I don't help you become better...I just help you create the same experiences."

Sophia nodded in agreement because Miss Ariel believed in coaching pageant contestants from the inside out, and the only way she could accomplish this was to get into Sophia's head and "cut through the cobwebs" as she put it. The more she helped Sophia resolve her fears while preparing for this pageant, the easier it would be for Sophia to see herself as the winner of this pageant. Because of all the fears that Sophia had been dealing with, tackling this one was the most significant challenge yet. This was just one of the reasons that Sophia loved working with Miss Ariel, because the advice she gave her went far beyond her pageant preparation and assisted her with life tools that she could use in any situation.

"Sophia," she heard Miss Ariel say as she turned her attention back to her pageant lesson. "I would like you to close your eyes and think about a very happy time in your life that you shared with your mom. Something that was so special, that every time you think about it, this occasion brings a smile to your face." Sophia closed her eyes and tried to think of something but she drew a blank. She could not perform under pressure, so Sophia remained quiet and just searched her memory for anything. After several moments Sophia opened her eyes and shook her head and replied, "I got nothin'."

Miss Ariel smiled and giggle lightly, "That's because you're trying too hard," she said. "Don't remember with your head Sophia, remember with your *heart*." Sophia shook her head again and said, "I can't. I'm afraid that I will cry." Miss Ariel looked thoughtfully at Sophia and remained quiet. "I'm afraid that if I say it out loud then it means that mom is never coming back. If I talk about her like she isn't here, then..." Sophia lowered her head in her hands and began to cry. Miss Ariel remained silent and waited for Sophia to regain composure, then asked her. "Sophia, you needed to cry to release that fear because you know that your mom is not coming back in the form that you remembered her as. It doesn't mean that she no longer exists."

Sophia looked puzzled because Miss Ariel was talking about her mom's spirit rather than her memory. Miss Ariel continued, "Sophia if you recall one great memory that you shared with your mom and rather than fear your emotions, celebrate them by celebrating them with the judges, then it may keep you from crying. If you change your perspective from being sad about one of the happiest memories you have of your mom and turned it into remembering the happiness you both shared, then you are in fact celebrating that moment. Close your eyes and feel the happiness you shared with her, and then tell me about the moment."

Sophia wiped the tears off her cheeks and took in a deep breath. She closed her eyes as Miss Ariel instructed, then pulled the memory and the emotions of that memory into her heart. As she remembered what it felt like to feel happy with her mom and the sound of her mom's voice as they laughed and talked together, then Sophia began to smile. The memory of this experience brought chills to Sophia and the more she remembered the details, the easier it was to remember her mom's touch as she held Sophia's hand, her voice as they laughed together, and her energy. Before Sophia knew it she was smiling ear to ear.

"Now," said Miss Ariel. "I would like you to share that memory with me while telling me why you want to win this pageant and how you can make a difference." As Sophia began sharing the memory of an afternoon with her mom that was one of the last one's she had before her mom get too sick to leave her bed. Sophia relived the experience through her memory, her voice got enthusiastic about the silly and fun moments and then turned solemn during the serious moments. Just as she was trained by Miss Ariel, Sophia transitioned her story and began to take her cause of breast cancer awareness to the level that "winners are made from," as Miss Ariel said while applauding her performance. "That was wonderful Sophia," she cheered then continued, "Now did you at any time while sharing that story with me, have the urge or need to begin crying?"

Sophia looked at Miss Ariel in awe and nodded, because she was so wrapped up in the emotions of happiness that for the first time since making the decision to enter the pageant, Sophia felt empowered. She leaned over and wrapped her arms around Miss Ariel who returned her embrace enthusiastically. "You can do this Sophia," Miss Ariel whispered in her ear. "You can win this pageant to celebrate your mom and help other people stay healthy and alive through your message. I know you can do it, and now you know it too." Sophia had not felt this good inside of her spirit since before her mom's death, actually since the moment of the experience that Sophia shared with Miss Ariel.

'Thank you so much," Sophia said. "I haven't felt this good in a long time, and the more I work with you the more I think I can do really well in this pageant." Miss Ariel smiled and said to Sophia, "I want to ask you the same question that I asked you when you first came to me over a month ago. How far do you want to get in this pageant journey you are on?" Sophia sat back and thought about it, as the last time Miss Ariel asked her this was on her first session. At that time Sophia remembers telling Miss Ariel that she wanted to do well in the pageant by sharing her mom's story and not falling on her face on stage.

Now that she has been working with Miss Ariel almost every day for the past 6 weeks, the idea of winning the pageant was becoming more of a reality. Sophia was beginning to see herself as someone who would be a great role model to other young people, but now she was seeing herself as an advocate as well. Despite her young age, Sophia understood that she had suffered the pain of loss of her mom but she also recognized that through this time she had grown, and through every moment was slowly healing. The idea that she could teach others to do the same was encouraging to Sophia and now she could see herself playing a bigger role through this process.

"Miss Ariel," Sophia said as she looked intensely in her eyes. "I want to win this pageant. I don't know if I will, but for the first time I think I can do this. What I mean is that I believe that I have the courage and the strength to make a difference, and I really want to try." As Sophia proceeded she noticed Miss Ariel lean back on her chair and listen to her. "Miss Ariel, there are so many girls who are prettier than I am, and some who are smarter than me. I am also acutely aware that I have never entered a pageant so I am competing with girls my age who have been in pageants since they were children. Since I have the best pageant coach," she stopped and smiled at Miss Ariel who returned the smile and giggled.

"You have also taught me that we are not defined by our experiences, but instead we can *redefine* ourselves each and every day *through* our thoughts, emotions, and actions. I don't know how the pageant will turn out, but I know that I don't want to settle for anything less than giving 100%. My goal is to win the state pageant so I can spread my message to people in this state and hopefully compete at Nationals sharing my message on a higher level. Do you think that I can accomplish this?" Sophia asked.

Miss Ariel tilted her head and studied Sophia as she replied, "I think the more important question is do *you* think you can accomplish this? Sophia this is all about you, and remembering what your journey was in this pageant. You are not creating the experience from beginning to end, but you are in fact remembering being at the end and remembering how you got there. You have already created this pageant journey, but you don't remember how you did it." Sophia's stared at her and replied, "Miss Ariel, you're making my head hurt."

Miss Ariel laughed and sat back up in her chair as she looked intently at Sophia and said. "Sophia when I told you that I coach from the inside out, I meant that in the literal sense. I view us as spiritual beings having a physical experience, so if this is what my belief is, then it only makes sense that as spiritual beings we are all energy and nothing separates energy from itself, not even by time. The *perception* of separation is what keeps us unaware of the steps we take in our journey until we are standing on the cobblestone path trying to decide which way to move. You are standing on the path of your pageant journey and are trying to remember if you chose to win, make the list of finalists, or share your experience and celebrate your mom's life through your immediate group of friends."

Even though Sophia understood what Miss Ariel was saying, she was still having a great deal of doubt as to how this pageant experience was supposed to end. Sophia was raised by wise parents who taught her to think outside of the box, but there was still something within Sophia that didn't feel quite right. "Miss Ariel," Sophia said. "I understand how I can share my message with the pageant world and even with people who aren't in pageants. What I don't understand is why I am still feeling anxious? I know I can be a good role model but what if nobody wants to listen to me? What if the girls in the pageant are mean to me or worse yet, if I do well in the pageant and possibly win, what if everyone else then doesn't like me because they think I am pretentious and mean?"

Miss Ariel interrupted her and said, "What do you mean by that Sophia? Who do you think will be mean to you and why would they be mean to you because you won a pageant?" Sophia knew this was Miss Ariel's way of making Sophia getting comfortable being uncomfortable because Miss Ariel very rarely asked Sophia a question that she didn't already know the answer to. She was 'leading the interview' as she explained to Sophia many times during their mock interview sessions.

Sophia sighed and replied, "I'm afraid that the girls in the pageant are mostly mean girls who are stuck up and think they are perfect. I guess I'm also afraid that my friends won't like me anymore if I win." Even though Sophia knew these thoughts swirled constantly in her head, she was surprised to hear herself say them out loud.

"Momma wanted to do pageants but said that only the mean girls do well, and I am not mean." Sophia said but was interrupted once again by Miss Ariel. "Sophia," Miss Ariel said. "I know that you are not a mean girl, then why are you entering a pageant? Either you believe that these pageants are for mean girls or you believe that they aren't...which one is it?" Sophia paused and considered Miss Ariel's question. "I'm not sure," she replied. Miss Ariel then responded by saying, "that will be your homework assignment to find out before our next session tomorrow won't it?"

Miss Ariel smiled and winked at Sophia as she gathered her papers and put her competition heels into her tote bag. Sophia always felt good when she left her pageant lesson and even as she hugged Miss Ariel good-bye, Sophia turned and said. "Miss Ariel, I hope you don't think I am being judgmental about pageants...it's just that...I don't know, maybe I *am* being judgmental." As Miss Ariel helped Sophia gather the rest of her belongings she stopped and stared at Sophia in silence for several very uncomfortable moments. Just when Sophia thought Miss Ariel had lost her mind she noticed her eyes filling with tears. "I think this is the time," Miss Ariel said. "Stay here Sophia, I have something for you."

As Sophia waited for Miss Ariel to return she wondered what must have been going through her head for her to react in the manner that she did. A few minutes later Miss Ariel appeared and had both of her hands behind her back. "Sophia," she said in a gentle voice. "I need you to sit down for a moment while I tell you something." As Sophia sat down she began to worry that something was terribly wrong with Miss Ariel. "Before I began working with you, I started having a feeling that something amazing was about to happen. I didn't know what it was, but there was just an energy that I was sensing that made me excited and when I met you I felt the energy get stronger."

Listening to Miss Ariel's words made Sophia less anxious because she at least ruled out that something bad was happening to Miss Ariel. "One evening after you went home from your pageant lesson, I had a dream. In my dream a beautiful woman came to me and told me that I was going to change the life of a young girl. Someone who was scared and broken inside." As Miss Ariel spoke, her hands began to tremble and tears filled her eyes once again. "This woman in my dream was wearing a beautiful pink flowing gown and looked like a model. She said to have an open heart and an open mind and then she handed me a letter. She said that I would know who this letter belonged to and I would also know when would be the proper time to give it to this person. Anyway, I woke up as soon as she handed me the letter in my dream. As I sat up and turned on my lamp Sophia, I noticed a small pink envelope lying on the table next to my bed."

Sophia stared at Miss Ariel as her heart beat louder and faster and she watched as Miss Ariel's handed Sophia a small pink envelope. The words *Sophia Rose* were written on the front of the envelope with her mom's handwriting. This was too much to take, and Sophia broke down into tears. As Miss Ariel pulled Sophia towards her she held her closely and said, "I'm sorry Sophia, I never meant to scare you or freak you out but I was freaked out!" Sophia's cry turned into laughter because Miss Ariel had always been so proper that she would have never thought she could utter those words.

They both wiped their own tears as they laughed nervously together, and just then Sophia realized Miss Ariel wasn't trembling anymore. What was more interesting is that Sophia smelled the scent of roses around them both. "Do you smell that?" Sophia asked. Miss Ariel sighed and replied, "Sophia since the day you walked into my office I have smelled roses during our sessions. The moment you leave, the scent is gone, but I never said anything because you didn't so I thought that maybe I was imagining that. As the sessions progressed, I enjoyed the smell so I was just thankful that it was a smell or roses rather than kitty litter."

They both laughed again and Sophia carefully placed the letter in her tote, and as she was walking out the door Miss Ariel said. "Sophia, I don't know the purpose of your journey, but what I do know is that someone who loves you very much wants desperately for you to know that you are not alone." She smiled and Sophia ran to Miss Ariel and gave her a warm embrace. "Thank you Miss Ariel," Sophia said as she turned around and ran out the door. As Sophia jumped in the car, she leaned over and kissed her dad on the cheek. He smiled and said, "That must have been one good pageant lesson."

When they got home, her dad informed Sophia that he had a business dinner that evening but they would stop by their favorite restaurant and order dinner to go. Although they both ate very healthy, Sophia was allowed to cheat and have pizza night one day out of the week if she needed comfort food. Tonight she felt like it would be a celebration rather than needing the pizza for comfort. As they arrived at the house and Sophia locked the door behind her, she waved from the window to her dad who waved back and then drove off to his business dinner.

Sophia reached into her tote bag and with pure excitement pulled out the letter in the pink envelope that Miss Ariel handed her earlier that evening. She sat down and listened as her heart raced in excitement, and as she opened the envelope and pulled out the letter, Sophia noticed the scent of roses began to fill the air. She smiled and began reading the letter slowly.

My Dearest Sophia,

Avoid the Blame Game

Life is such a beautiful gift, yet so many souls take each and every day for granted. Parents work so hard at protecting and educating their children about life, and children learn from their influences which help develop the core of their foundation. Because children are like sponges, they absorb everything around them whether it is a positive or negative influence. Sophia, you are such a bright child with a brilliant light that surrounds you. From the "other side," each and every one of you are intelligent and brilliant souls, yet with the experiences that scar your emotions or tarnish your faith you grow further away from your authentic self.

When you enter this world, you learn from those around you who have also learned their opinions and developed their character from their parents and influences around them. You soon realize that the lessons your parents teach you are learned from the lessons their parents have learned and taught them. As parents, we want so much to influence our children in a positive manner, but we are still very much humans and make mistakes. Learn to forgive us for those mistakes, because you will eventually be asking the same from your own children.

One of the beautiful truths about your journey through life is that you will make mistakes and you will learn from them and move on, or you will choose to repeat them and include them into your life. As your parents Daddy and I made mistakes in the name of love, because we either felt we were doing what was best for you or what we felt was best for us. Either way we learned from you, and you learned from us. Now if you choose to repeat mistakes that you learned from us and know in your heart that you are remaining in a place of fear, then you need to be responsible and own your actions.

Let me give you an example of this because children from the age of three to ninety three practice this blame game throughout their lives until they choose to know better. From the earliest age I can remember, you have always been fearless and loved adventures. I on the other hand was always afraid of the "what if..." what if this doesn't happen or what if that does happen. I chose to remain in fear for most of my life because I learned from my mother to be in fear of what we cannot control. Rather than choosing to examine my fears and their origins, I allowed them to become a part of my life while passing them on to you as well.

Remember the day you wanted to compete in your very first pageant and Daddy and I told you that you were too young to compete? My fears of being judged and not adding up to another person's expectations caused me to introduce those fears to you by no fault of your own. The truth is that you were a little too young to compete in the mindset that you were in, but I failed to help you prepare to get into a healthier mindset so you could take one step towards your dream.

Instead, I tried to convince you that pageants were a place where mean girls competed against each other and the judges would tell you that you were not pretty enough, smart enough, or talented enough. These were actually my fears when I wanted to compete in a pageant myself, and I talked myself out of it every year until I finally gave up on my dream of ever winning a beauty pageant. As your mother, I was transferring my fears to you by teaching you that pageantry was a negative thing. Since you were so young and influenced by me, you began to adopt those same fears that were always mine, but you made them your own.

Now that you are grieving and your soul desires to connect with itself in love, you are still living your life through my fears rather than releasing them and creating your life from doing what you love. This is a choice that you must be disciplined in breaking, because it no longer serves you and it never did. It served me and my fears which I inadvertently passed on to you. Every experience that you choose to create in your life serves to connect you more with your soul on a level of love or fear. If you choose to connect to your soul in love then the result is that you connect to God on that level. If you choose to connect your soul to fear, then you disconnect from Source energy because love and fear cannot coexist in the same emotion. The stronger emotion will always prevail, so you must be deliberate about creating your life in love.

I have experienced adopting another's fear and owning them as my own, yet I blamed the other person who taught me these fears as if they were at fault. Owning your decisions and thoughts is your responsibility, so if you are serving something that creates fear in your life, release it now. The law of free will does not place blame on your thoughts, emotions, and actions onto another. You must be aware of what you have chosen to adopt as your own, and what your own truth is so you can decipher each of these beliefs. Release illusions from your life so you can continue living a life of love and joy. Question those beliefs that don't feel right and examine them carefully before you choose to create more life experiences from them.

If these illusions or false beliefs are another person's then replace them with the truth that you know is right. If you have doubt, then pray and allow God to show you what is truth and what is illusion in your life. Realize though that once you know something to be truth, you are responsible for the gift of knowing. Even if you choose not to acknowledge something as truth, and are pretending that it serves you then your soul knows and you must listen to your soul. For it is Gods way of communicating with you, and by keeping the lines of communication open then you grow your relationship with Him.

I am so proud of the girl you are and the woman that you are becoming. Always know that I am only a thought away.

I love you forever,

Momma

You Will See When You Believe
Chapter 21

Sophia opened her eyes to her bedroom filled with sunlight and she felt warmth in her heart that she had not realized before. It felt as if something in her heart was healing because normally Sophia was accustomed to waking up to the feeling of sadness and aching in her heart. Sophia had noticed that as the month's progressed the aching was beginning to dissipate. This morning felt different because for the first tie Sophia felt a relief of the pain and what was more interesting is that the ache was actually replaced with a feeling of love and joy.

This feeling elated Sophia because since she had not experienced joy in such a long time, the feeling was more magnified and this joy felt even more beautiful. It felt as if she had numbed her senses for so long that the sheer feeling of happiness was intensified like never before, and she appreciated feeling good whereas before it was an emotion that she merely took for granted. Sophia took in a deep breath and closed her eyes just to relish in the beauty of the morning.

She was excited to talk to Miss Ariel this afternoon for her pageant lesson because Sophia wanted to take the feeling of this joy and see how far she could expand it. Sophia opened her eyes and sat upright as the she had the realization that she wanted to win this pageant. No longer did she want to settle for what she perceived others as wanting for her, but now she wanted for herself the feeling of being accepted by herself for the imperfect and struggling soul that she was. For the first time Sophia wanted to embrace and accept herself for all that she had learned from her mom's battle with cancer and everything she learned about life, death, and the ability to smile again.

Later that afternoon as Sophia met with Miss Ariel she explained these emotions and goals with her. After realizing that she wanted to win to expand more feelings of happiness, Miss Ariel listened intently and smiled as she realized that whatever the contents of that letter had, Sophia was experiencing hope for the very first time since her mom passed away. Sophia rambled on about her new emotions and that she just knew if she won the pageant then she would feel even more joyous, and Sophia wanted to embrace these feelings.

After Sophia explained her new goal, Miss Ariel remained silent and studied Sophia for several seconds then said, "Sophia I am so proud of you. Realizing that you have a desire to experience a new journey through pageantry is a big accomplishment for you." Miss Ariel paused and selected her words carefully, "have you considered what would happen if you don't win?' Sophia frowned and responded, "what do you mean?'

Miss Ariel folded her hands together and proceeded, "I mean what if you continue working hard at preparing for the pageant and you don't win? What will you experience then? Will you be happy for your progress that you have made so far or will you become depressed again with another feeling of loss?' Sophia was shocked by Miss Ariel's questions but considered them carefully before responding. "I hadn't thought about that," she replied. "I guess I never considered the feeling of losing a pageant being the same as the feeling of losing my mom."

Miss Ariel paused then said, "Sophia they are two *extremely* different feelings of sorrow and emotions but loss is loss, and are you prepared to not allow yourself to delve into depression if you don't win the pageant because the feeling of depression was once familiar to you?" Sophia began to understand Miss Ariel's questioning and looked away as she sat quietly with her arms folded in front of her. She had started out this conversation feeling such excitement and Miss Ariel suddenly popped her bubble of happiness with one little question.

"I think I'll be fine," Sophia finally said. "After all it is just a beauty pageant, it's not like it is the cure to cancer I am competing for." Sophia's response took them both by surprise and Miss Ariel responded by laughing and nodding in agreement. After their laughter subsided, Sophia hesitated and then added, "Miss Ariel, for the first time since momma died I feel as if there is a happy place in my heart. Something that is giving me a goal to look forward to, and I just want to embrace this feeling as long as I can. I don't know if I will win or come in last place, but I know there is something so deep inside me that is focused on winning this pageant that I need to believe I can do it."

Miss Ariel looked thoughtfully at Sophia and waited for her to continue. "I know that I can't control who is competing or what the judges want in a winner, but what I can control is how I prepare for this pageant and that's what I want to remain focused on. I had a dream one night that momma was smiling at me holding a scepter and a robe and she is waiting for me at the end of a dark stage. She didn't speak to me but just waited for me with a smile on her face. Miss Ariel, I know that momma is still around me, and as crazy as it sounds I feel her with me sometimes. Not physically, but I feel her energy just like I did when she was alive."

Sophia paused and waited for any response from Miss Ariel who just sat quietly listening to her speak. Sophia continued, "I believe there is something special about this pageant and I don't know what it is but I have to give it everything I have so I am not left wondering and wishing that I had trusted my heart. Does any of this make sense?" Miss Ariel nodded and said, "Yes, Sophia this makes complete sense and thank you for trusting me enough to share your dream with me. Let me ask you something? Do you remember how this pageant journey ends?"

Miss Ariel's question surprised Sophia and she couldn't hold back her shocked expression. "What do you mean how this ends?" Sophia responded. Miss Ariel shifted in her seat and explained, "Sophia when I won an International Pageant, I prepared for it much the same as I am preparing you for your state pageant. However I added an element of the subconscious in my pageant preparation. Since so much of achieving any goal is mental and emotional, I challenged myself mentally as much as I did physically in the gym. Every night I would visualize myself winning the pageant, but rather than creating the feeling of winning, I remembered what that feeling was so I could work backwards."

Still somewhat confused Sophia asked, "How can you remember something that hasn't happened yet?" Miss Ariel smiled and said, "By removing the illusion of separation from my goal. I had allowed my mind to deceive me into believing that I was trying to create an experience, so I changed my perspective and reminded myself the experience already happened. Since winning the pageant already felt so real to me then I only had to remind myself of the feelings I had when I won, how the hot stage lights felt on my skin, and how I could only hear my heart beating right before my name was announced. Remembering this process allowed it to become easier for me to my brain to grasp this intangible goal was already realized. Do you want me to teach you how to do it?" Miss Ariel asked.

Sophia nodded in excitement and for the next several hours they practiced this remembering exercise to the extent that Sophia felt comfortable enough to do it by herself every evening before she went to bed. Sophia made a commitment that she would dedicate her time to developing her mental preparation as diligently as she developed her muscle tone at the gym for the fitness portion of the competition. One of the things Sophia loved about Miss Ariel was that she thought differently about many situations and had a knack for helping Sophia understand things that she might not normally comprehend.

Later that afternoon Sophia was excited to share with her dad about the remembering exercise that Miss Ariel had taught her. She explained how the process works when setting goals that it is easier for the mind to remember achieving the goal and review how she was able to achieve it rather than creating the goal step by step as if it never existed. "So let me get this straight," he dad chimed in. "If I remember winning the lottery then my mind will create the winning lottery numbers?" he asked while chuckling. "No Daddy," Sophia replied. "Well....I suppose if you really wanted to win the lottery and knew in your heart that you had a deep calling to do so then I suppose it could be true." Sophia replied.

She thought for a few second s then added, "Miss Ariel explained that whatever goal your heart is set on achieving, you still have to create it in thought, emotion, and action. Since my goal is to win this pageant, then I have to add those elements into remembering achieving my goal so I can work backwards. She showed me methods of remembering being the titleholder so I can add all sorts of elements into it and make the goal as tangible as possible. Miss Ariel walked me through this step by step and by the time we were done, then I really *felt* as if I won the pageant!"

Sophia's dad smiled and was beyond pleased that she was finally excited about something in her life, and if winning a beauty pageant was the goal first on the list then he would support and encourage her every step of the way. Sophia's dad and mom had impressed upon her all of her life that any goal was attainable, and she just had to focus her efforts on that goal until she achieved it. The word *impossible* was never used in their home let alone anyone uttering the words "I can't," as that caused a family meeting to teach Sophia the difference between illusion and reality. Illusion is where a person's experiences were created from fear and reality is here their experiences were deliberately created in love and passion.

230

Later that evening Sophia was practicing her mock judge's interview with a group of her friends who lived in her neighborhood. As they each lined up a chair in front of her, Sophia then got to practice interview questions with them. These questions ranged anything from how she would stop bullying, to what advice she would give a new contestant competing in a pageant, and one "judge" even asked her to explain her thoughts on health care reform. Just as Sophia and Miss Ariel had practiced, she answered her questions with thoughtfulness, sincerity, and great eye contact. Miss Ariel would have been proud.

As they were wrapping up thirty minutes of intensive mock interviews combined with serious and not so serious questions, Sophia's closest friend Crystal chirped up and asked abruptly, "Sophia you don't expect to win this pageant just because your mom died do you?" Sophia turned suddenly and stared at Crystal. Shock and confusion kept Sophia from saying a word. The room became so quiet you could hear the breathing of everyone in it and finally Sophia said, "I can't believe you just said that to me."

Crystal just stared blankly back at Sophia and continued. "It's just that there are a lot of girls in this pageant, and some of them have been competing in pageants since they were little girls. There's a rumor that you just want the judges to feel sorry for you because your mom died and let's face it Sophia, nobody can compete against a sad story like yours." Just then Sophia's other friend Jennifer spoke up and suggested that Crystal's comment was not only rude but uncalled for. After all Sophia had been preparing for this pageant for months and she was working just as hard if not harder than some of the other seasoned pageant contestants.

As the girls put their chairs away and munched on popcorn and snacks while watching pageant videos on the internet, Sophia couldn't help but be broken hearted. She couldn't believe that Crystal was supposed to be her friend and would say something so mean to her, and it scared her more that others were thinking the same thing. Being the gracious hostess that her mom had raised her to be Sophia hid her hurt feelings with smiles and thanks as the last of her mock judges panel walked out the door and ran to their homes in the neighborhood.

"How did it go?" asked Sophia's dad as he entered the kitchen where Sophia was wiping down the counters with a damp dish towel. All of the excitement that Sophia had been experiencing throughout the day went out the door with Crystal's comment. As Sophia explained to her dad the events that unfolded with her friends, she watched his face as it became hardened. His eyes shot an angry expression but he held his anger and bit his tongue to ensure not to say what he wanted to say. Sophia noticed the longer her dad remained silent, the more flushed his face became. "Daddy, "she finally spoke up. "Do you think that the judge's would only vote for me because momma died?"

All of the hard work and feeling of accomplishment began to fade and for the first time Sophia's dad found himself having to defend his daughter to another teenager. As they both sat down at the kitchen table, Sophia noticed that her dad was beginning to calm himself as his face softened and he took a deep breath before speaking. "Sophia, what do you think

Crystal's motivation was to say something so hurtful to you? Why do you think she said that?" Sophia remembered the conversations they often had when they discussed other people and how they either uplifted another person or destroyed them through their words. Her dad would always tell her behind every word was a motivation and her job through life was to understand the motivation before believing the words as truth or illusion.

Sophia wondered but wasn't sure why Crystal who had been her friend throughout her mom's illness and finally her death, would say something so mean. "I don't know Daddy, but the pageant is in a few days and I don't want the judges to think that I am trying to get them to feel sorry for me. " Sophia looked down with sadness in her eyes and then looked back at her dad and continued, "Daddy should I be competing in this pageant? I know I wanted to make a difference but what if I am going to just be felt sorry for. I don't know what to do."

Sophia's dad studied her for a moment then said, "I think that you need to sleep on it and make a decision in the morning. This is your journey and I will never force you to compete in a pageant when your heart doesn't feel called to do so. If you wake up and know in your heart that you are not meant to enter this pageant then I will support your decision fully. If however you decide that you still want to compete and are afraid of what others will think, then let's find a way to work through that Sophia but this ultimately has to be your decision." Sophia nodded in agreement and gave her dad a hug before going to bed.

"Daddy thank you for being so supportive...I love you." Sophia kissed him on the forehead and went upstairs for bed. After she showered and said a prayer before going to bed, she crawled into bed and opened her nightstand drawer open to pull out her bible. Sophia had not opened this book since before her mom passed away, and as she opened the book she noticed some of the pages had been dog eared when she had found scriptures that inspired her or touched her heart. Opening some of the pages that she had marked, Sophia began reading the verses and continued perusing through the book until she noticed a page with thicker corners folded back. As she opened the page a small pink envelope laid in between the thin pages of her bible. On the front of the envelope were the words *Sophia Rose* written with the beautiful handwriting of her mom.

Sophia smiled and began to open the envelope and as tears filled her eyes, Sophia wiped them away and began to read the letter...

My Dearest Sophia,

You Will See When You Believe

What is it that you want? When you lie awake at night and are left alone with only your thoughts and emotions, what is it that knocks at the front door of your soul just waiting to be created? Have you allowed yourself to dream and truly given yourself permission to be happy? Sophia, your soul longs to experience love from self in ways you have not yet allowed yourself to love. You look around those who fill the world with you and place the same expectations of happiness and the same barriers only to have the same results in your life. Rather than questioning whether or not these people are happy, you automatically imitate their lives as if their path leads to the only happy road...yet when you look at them, are they actually happy?

Why not try something new for the first time in your life, and dedicate yourself to recreating yourself and taking your soul to the highest level every moment you exist. If you awoke every morning and refused to step foot out of bed until you felt gratitude, then you would experience life in a very different way. Instead, you hit the alarm clock, groan, roll over and dread getting up in the morning. This is the time when your body has rested and your spirit is ready to create your journey through this life, so it should be celebrated. After all, you woke up this morning and knew you had another moment to celebrate love through your life. Take control of those moments because life is so precious and so short, there is not one second on this journey through life that is promised to anyone.

God places you here in this journey, through this illusion to allow you to know and grow into yourself. You are experiencing this beautiful awakening so that you can understand the truth of who you are and the perfection that you possess just by being you! If you only knew the magnitude of love that is held for each and every soul that travels on this journey through life, you would be overwhelmed. Yet, so many days you walk this journey feeling alone and lonely when there are millions of souls united on the other side, helping you through your struggles and sending you light and love. Many of these souls you have traveled through your life with at some point, and many have known you from being a part of your complete energy. Remember that the arms and legs do not see each other every moment of their journey, but they are all very much connected to the same whole.

If you could look at your life without limits, then what is it that you want to create? Pilots, artists, and teachers all had dreams of becoming what they already were, and when they listened to their soul's calling then they were awakened into that which they were meant to be. Stop searching for your answers to your own journey in the world outside of yourself, rather take those moments gifted to you to discover who you are and what you want to experience. When you take advice from lost and lonely souls, then you learn from that advice how to be lost and lonely as well.

You have had a dream to inspire others and to heal the world one soul at a time, and one day my child you will do just that. Dreams knock on the doors of your soul because they were placed there by your Creator, so stop closing the doors to them or you risk eventually forgetting that you own the key to release them and set them free. Respect the journey of the souls traveling their path on the road with you, but don't choose to set your dreams aside in order to help them believe in theirs. The world is filled with so many dreamers who have forgotten where they placed their lost dreams. Yet these souls have failed to recognize that as they owned the power to close the door on their dreams, they too own the power to open that door once again.

Live by faith in what you don't yet see but know to be real, and what you believe in you will eventually see in your experience. Whether your goal is to get good grades in school or become captain of your dance team, believe in the power of your dreams and remember that every dream you have is to be respected and treasured. Nobody has the power to take away a dream, but the dreamer has the power to relinquish their dreams for another. When you deceive yourself, you disempower yourself and life is about empowering and owning your right to be loved.

You began reading these letters reluctantly and as you allowed your heart to connect with your spirit once again, you now understand that these lessons are as real as the words on the pages of a book. Words are energy and are used to create and destroy, so choose your words carefully and always be aware of how you speak to yourself and to others. The bible refers to the world being created through God's words Realize that words have created and destroyed lives for thousands of years, so create your experiences with words that reflect the legacy you want to leave behind for others to read 100 years from now.

I commend your faith and allowing yourself to be open to my love and my words, because although I am not with you in body I am always with you in spirit. I know this is why our communication was so important, because it serves a greater role than the two of us. Our journey together serves as a constant reminder to those who needed it, that nothing separates the love of a mother from her child... not in life and not in death. God's words are gentle reminders that love is the Source of our connection to one another, whether we are family or strangers. There are so many souls here on this side of heaven that try to awaken the hearts of their loved ones, and they visit them in dreams and send signs to these broken-hearted souls. They will never stop trying to show them that they are with them every step of the journey even though they cannot see their loved ones anymore

Since we are all connected through love, one God, one Source, one energy, then how can we possibly be separate? If you remember that the perception of separateness is what keeps you alone in the pain of your grief, then take notice of those gentle reminders your loved ones send you along your day. Whether it is a yellow butterfly that crosses your path just when you are thinking about your loved one, or a person who shares the same name or similar physical features as the person you lost, there are no such things as coincidences. Everything has a purpose under the heavens.

What may have separated you from another in life through fear is replaced by love in their physical passing, so it becomes a greater challenge to connect with those loved ones left behind if they are still in the perception of fear. If someone was ill when they crossed over to the hands of God, they are no longer in that sick body and mind. They are dancing and free from any physical barriers, so needless to say – there are a lot of dancing souls on this side of heaven! They are striving to reach their loved ones to let them know they are experiencing love greater than one could ever imagine. Reach these souls through your words and have enough faith in the power of God that you are good enough to perform your calling.

Let every soul be reminded that although they may walk through their journey of life feeling lonely, they are never alone. Children are sending signs through teddy bears, boys are leaving baseball gloves in odd places, and parents are sending roses to their children. Animals that have crossed over are sending their favorite toys and even other animals that need rescuing in the physical realm. There are signs everywhere and these recipients of those signs are so immersed in their own pain that they often fail to recognize them. The teddy bears are being placed gently back on the bed from where they fell, the baseball gloves are being placed back on the shelves and the smell of roses becomes just a figment of someone's imagination. The stray animals are being left on the streets and the dog toys are being given away without notice of why they were even discovered.

Grief has a way of overwhelming the heart and soul of the person left behind as it almost did you my child. Your mission lies beyond pageants and celebrating life, as does every person who walks the face of this earth journey. It becomes so easy for society to judge another from their own limited perception and fear based thinking, that they often disregard so many souls' purposes. What if the homeless man on the street whose loyal German Shepherd sitting next to him, was sent to remind a mother that the child she lost is safe in the hands of his Creator with the German Shepherd dog who had passed away years before him. What if the unruly child in the grocery store line was acting up because she was a spitting image of the daughter who had been taken all too soon from a grieving mother. Yet rather than look up into that child's eyes, the mother standing behind them grows more irritated and moves to another line?

What if the journey of the professional athlete whose career was cut short due to a drinking and driving conviction had a greater calling, that aimed towards the high school star that was cutting out of school to party and was driving home intoxicated before his parents returned home. What If that act from the professional athlete had saved this young boys life as well as the life of his friends? Yet on this journey through life, people look at the journey of another and judge it rather than learn from the many lessons being shown all around us. There are only perfect souls having imperfect experiences, and these souls are not to be judged because nobody knows the agreement they had with God before their birth.

Take the time and energy that you spend judging and condemning another, and work your cause and your agreement with God so at the end of your journey, you know you did everything you had intended to do. Judge not, believe in the unbelievable, and know that every day is a pure gift. Rather than discovering ways to be disappointed in others, look for ways that you can inspire and empower others. Come from a place of contribution and give your gifts rather than waiting to receive the gifts from others.

When you believe in your dreams enough, you will see those dreams manifest into your experience. Rather than looking for excuses not to try, reach for the impossible and if you fall short, then stand up again, wipe off your knees, and try again. As a matter of fact, continue trying until you have exhausted all of your different options and if those fail you, then continue listening to the voice of God and learn to do things differently than before so you can get the results that are different than before. Trust your instincts, love greater than you have ever loved before, and be in an attitude of gratitude.

Hold your head up high and never allow another to make you feel inferior, because those who try to condemn are also just as broken as you are. Nobody is perfect, or more important than you are so never place your dreams on the back burner for another just because you don't feel your dreams are as worthy. Give love to others without expecting it in return and above all Sophia...know that you are walking with others in this journey through life because you are the chosen one. Everyone who walks this journey through life is the chosen one or they would not be here. Respect and honor your role for God and show the same to those around you.

You have believed in the unbelievable and have allowed your heart to open to the truth of my existence. Your faith has healed your broken heart and you are able to move forward now as a teacher and a student. Now that you believe what you do not see, you will soon see evidence of what you have believed. I am so proud of you, and am honored to be your momma. I visit you in your sleep and watch you breathe just as I used to do when you were a baby, because no matter how old you are you will always be my baby. My connection to you has only grown from this side, and as you have witnessed, we are still able to have a relationship like we have never experienced before.

Always remember that I am only a thought away. When you need to talk to me, then know I hear your thoughts and feel your emotions. You have felt my touch and my energy when I stand next to you, and you recognize the smell of roses just before you feel my presence. Sophia Rose, I named you because people used to say I looked like my favorite actress and roses have always been my favorite flower. I loved the smell of them and what they represented. Roses are given to others out of the intention of love, celebration, or encouragement, which is why the scent of roses always fills the room before you become aware of me.

Roses can create a strong emotion and can cause one to cry out of joy or sorrow. They are the universal flower of love and whenever a rose is given to another, the underlying tone of that gift is in essence love. Whether it is the love of friends, family, or strangers hoping to be in love, to me roses signify one common element...love.

As my daughter you have brought a greater love to me than you will ever know, and I waited my entire life for you. Leaving you and your father behind in your grief was not meant to hurt you, but rather to allow your spirit to grow. My agreement between God and myself had been fulfilled and I was ready to leave the physical realm. I am still assisting you in your life and serving as your guide from this side of heaven, but now I can grow in my spirit as well. Death is merely a separation of the physical body, but the emotions of grief continue to destroy lives of those left behind because they don't know what to believe in anymore.

Don't waste your time or energy trying to understand why I got sick and passed away, especially when you meet people on your journey who got sick and recovered fully. The illness was the death of my physical body, but the fulfillment of my agreement with God was the true cause of my leaving the physical realm and crossing over into spirit. You have learned not to judge because you don't know what the agreement was behind the lives of others and their agreement with God before their birth. My physical death may never make sense to you, but the truth of my life does so focus on that to continue healing. So much energy and so many sleepless nights are the result of people trying to make sense of death when on this side, the death of the body signifies the rebirth of the soul. It is a celebration here because now nothing separates me from being with you.

Believe in the truth that nothing separates the joining of two people through love, not in life and not in spirit. Believe in the healing process, and most of all believe that you are entitled to your birthright which is to experience love to its greatest extent. Live life beyond measure and know that you and I are connected forever. I am so proud of you my precious child and will always love you. Remember that I am just a thought away.

I love you forever,

Momma

Remembering Your "Why"
Chapter 22

When Sophia awoke she was still holding the letter in her hand with the open bible laying on her lap. She had fallen asleep after reading the letter and had not awakened once during the night. As Sophia held the letter in her right hand she closed her eyes and listened to her heart. She knew that all of the months of preparing for the pageant were not going to be wasted on Crystal's negativity or Sophia's fear. She said a prayer to release her fear of what others might think of her, and asked God that she be filled with strength and courage to complete this goal she had set out to accomplish.

After sharing with her dad that she had a restful sleep and was ready to compete, they both celebrated with her favorite breakfast of chocolate chip pancakes and extra crispy bacon and Sophia spent the remainder of the day packing her competition clothes and items for the pageant. Since they were supposed to leave for the pageant later that afternoon, Sophia wanted to be sure that she had everything she needed. After packing, Sophia got a manicure and pedicure and by the time her dad drove her to the hotel for the pageant orientation Sophia felt like a princess.

Because the pageant was in the same city Sophia lived in, she didn't have to travel as far as many of the other contestants from other parts of the state, so she felt refreshed and rested by the time they arrived. The pageant director sent out a letter with instructions that all of the contestants were to arrive to the hotel for orientation in their favorite red T-Shirt and blue denim shorts. Since they were allowed to wear their own selection of shoes, Sophia selected a pair of taupe wedges that highlighted her tall and thin frame and toned legs that she had worked so hard to develop from months with a personal trainer.

As she stepped out of the car with her make-up fresh and her long hair styled with beachy curls, Sophia felt like a million dollars and there was nothing anyone could say or do at this point to take this feeling away. That is until she walked through the hotel lobby and stepped behind another contestant with dark brown hair and a great tan. "Well hi Sophia," she heard a familiar voice say behind her, and as Sophia turned around to acknowledge the person who said hello, her heart skipped a beat as she saw Crystal smiling at her.

"Crystal?" Sophia said in a startled voice as she saw Crystal walking towards her wearing the same red T-Shirt and blue denim shorts all the contestants were required to wear. As a smug smile covered Crystal's face she said, "Surprise! I decided to compete this year." As Sophia watched Crystal walk past her and approach another group of girls, her anger grew. All of these mock interviews that Crystal had suggested they do to 'help' Sophia were in fact Crystal learning how to work a judge's interview room. The more Sophia thought about the past few weeks and then the comment Crystal made yesterday, the angrier she became. .

Sophia ran into the hotel bathroom and closed the door behind her as her anger turned to hurt, and she was wiping the tears from her eyes quickly so her makeup would not run and get ruined. Sophia couldn't believe that her friend would betray her like this because not only did she get to be trained by Sophia during these mock interviews, but she took her betrayal a step further by trying to make Sophia feel bad by saying that nasty comment. As Sophia stared in the mirror, she touched up her makeup and after applying her lip gloss, she pulled the envelope out of her pocket that she found in her bible last night and read it once again. It didn't matter what Crystal or anyone else thought about her competing because this pageant was about her and her mom, and nobody else mattered. This pageant was a celebration of life and the power of love from a mother to her child, no matter how that was shown.

Sophia smiled as she tucked the letter back into her pocket and before she walked out of the bathroom she said a prayer of strength and gratitude and took a deep breath. All of the years of watching her mom battle cancer, the chemo treatments, radiation, and moments of watching her mom cry as she began losing her hair flooded Sophia's memory. Sophia remembers the day her dad sat with her mom in front of the bathroom mirror and shaved her head because she could not stand waking up in the morning with clumps of her hair falling out and laying on her pillow case. Sophia remembers watching her mom cry as she felt a loss of her femininity and beauty fall to the floor with her long beautiful hair.

She was there to honor the days and weeks her mom suffered in silence with flu like symptoms after chemo treatments with vomiting and diarrhea and feeling miserable in bed. This pageant was about celebrating the rounds of radiation that burned and scarred her mom's delicate skin and the six hours of surgery with 5 different specialists who extended her life for 8 more months that Sophia could spend with her. This pageant was about honoring the countless patients, family, doctors, and loved ones who each and every day suffered in the fight against cancer.

The more Sophia thought about her "why" and the entire reason she decided to compete in this pageant, the less significant any comments or negativity from other people even mattered. Suddenly Sophia felt a burst of energy fill her heart and her spirit filled with such love that she no longer felt as if she were in this pageant alone. The scent of roses filled the air and as she looked in the mirror she saw, for the first time the beauty that filled her soul. Suddenly she looked in the mirror and saw the face of love and beauty reflecting back at her. The small blemishes that she once focused on faded and she saw the spirit of someone who wanted to make a difference.

The skin she focused on hiding with makeup now glowed in truth and love and for the first time, Sophia Rose saw the similarities in her that so many saw in her mother. She smiled and nodded to the reflection in the mirror and softly whispered, "Thank you momma, this one is for you."

You Own the Key
Chapter 23

The rhinestone crown glistened in the mirror as Sophia stared at her own reflection, barely having enough time to understand the events that just occurred. The blurry memories all came flooding back as she remembered standing on the large theatre stage, and holding the hands of two of her sister queens while they waited for the results to be tabulated. It felt as if just moments ago, Sophia was an ordinary young girl who nobody even noticed in the school hallways, and now she wore the coveted crown and title that would immediately throw her into the spotlight in the media and certainly throughout the country. As she heard the chatter of other contestants' voices in the theatre hallway, Sophia smiled at herself in the mirror and reached up to touch the ornate crown that sparkled with the slightest movement of her head.

"I did it..." she whispered to herself, "I actually did it." Despite her efforts, Sophia could not hold back the tears that welled in her eyes and slowly made their way down her rosy cheeks. These were tears of joy and sorrow, as her bittersweet moment would have been something that her late mother would have been so proud of her for accomplishing. Although Sophia lost her mom to breast cancer just one year ago, she knew that her mom would be so proud of her and there was not a doubt in Sophia's mind that her mother was watching her and sharing the same joyful and tearful moment from heaven. *What a journey,* she thought to herself as her mind recalled the memories that led her to compete in this pageant. Little did she know that what began as an effort to heal from the death of her mom, would lead down a road that would change her life forever.

It seems like only yesterday that Sophia was grieving from the loss of her mom and making every effort not to lose herself in the grips of depression and emotional aguish. Tonight she felt overwhelming joy and peace as she carried the same crown on her head that her mom had shown her in a dream just months before. What a bittersweet moment that was created from the depths of sorrow to now the dream of tomorrow, for Sophia realized that as an ordinary girl...she is very special in so many ways. Sophia has the gift of intuition and her gift was pushed to the limits this past year when she made the decision to travel a road that so few dare to take. Sophia chose to see beyond what her eyes could see, and created a dream so big that she knew she would cherish for the rest of her life.

The memory of her mom's death and the recollection of the journey she had just completed was too overwhelming for Sophia to take in, and she watched her reflection in the mirror become blurry as her big brown eyes could no longer hold back the tears, so they streamed uncontrollably down her face. As she dropped her head to her hands, Sophia caught sight of a small pink envelope peeking out of her purse. "Where did this come from?" she heard herself asking, but suddenly she realized that she was the only person left in the theatre dressing room her attention went back to the envelope. Sophia's trembling hand reached for the card and as she slowly opened it, a smile formed across her face. Her eyes read the words *Sophia Rose* on the envelope, and she knew this was a very special letter she was receiving. As she slowly opened the card, Sophia's heart began to race as she read the words, "My dearest Sophia..."

My Dearest Sophia,

You own the Key

We are nearing the end of your lessons and you are growing so much on your spiritual journey! I watch you now experiencing more moments of joy and allowing the light to permeate through to your spirit through those tiny open cracks that were once closed so tightly. Your moments of grieving are slowly being replaced with moments of gratitude and songs in your heart, and time is healing your heart each and every day. You have come to realize that you don't need to hold onto the pain of losing me in order to remain connected to me.

I speak for every momma who has ever lost a child, for every father who has ever experienced the life of someone they love being torn from their heart. I speak for those children who stand alone in their journey through life wondering what will happen to them now. My words reflect every son, every daughter, every parent, pet, or loved one who has ever loved and lost. They are all here on the other side with me trying to reach out to those they love and let them know that everything is going to be alright. These souls wander through their journey here trying to reach out to their loved ones and let them know that the signs and wonders they have been experiencing are in fact sent from them.

These souls try desperately to reconnect with their lost loves to help them heal their spirits so they don't waste another precious moment of their journey mourning the loss of those they loved. The dreams they share in the lonely and empty moments of their nights are in fact their loved ones reaching out to them in desperate attempt to let them know they are not gone but still by their side. These souls are the precious children of God who are all connected to you and me through the love of the Divine. We are all connected because we are all part of the same whole. God is the Source energy of all there is, and we experience our lives through Him and He experiences life through us.

There is no separation and no beginning without end, as we are all part of the same whole. Every soul who has experienced this journey through life is supporting the greater whole of the journey of every individual who is walking and will ever walk this journey. This is why conflict affects not only the person who is receiving it, but most importantly the person who is sending out the negative energy. This energy comes back to that same soul ten-times over because they are in fact sending out experiences through energy that is being received by them.

If you think about God being one "person" with no other person in existence, then we in essence are all a part of His heart, soul, and being. Some of us choose to experience being the "heart" of God while another may want to experience being the hand, or the feet of Him; all playing a significant role in the whole of God. With nothing else existing but God, then if the hand decides to strike out to the foot of God, the hand will experience the pain it sent out more than the foot that was struck. You cannot send out fear and pain to another without experiencing it yourself in greater force, because you came from deliberate intention.

This is why you must understand that you alone hold the key to your own ultimate happiness and experiences in life. Even though negative experiences occur and are often brought on by another, we have the power to control how we react to those experiences and what we choose to create from them. The person who chooses to experience the "feet" of God still has the power to make leaps and bounds across their journey and leave imprints in the sand that will enlighten and empower themselves and another. Just as the soul who is experiencing the "heart" of God has the power to mend from being broken and send out love to themselves and the Universe through intention and the use of their own gifts.

We are all part of the greater whole Sophia, and realize that as a part of the whole we each hold the key to open doors that have never been opened before. What oftentimes happens though is that we as souls travel through the same open door that another unlocked in their journey, and forget that our own life calling may be different than theirs. We don't need to be the same cookie cutter version of our parents or grandparents, but we can take the best parts of them and continue leaving our own imprint in our journey. Even though I was a teacher, doesn't mean that you too must become a teacher if your heart calls out to you to be an artist or a writer.

Because your father chose to experience his life in a certain profession doesn't mean that you too must follow that profession. All it means is that you have been exposed to the best and the worst of those professions, and you can make a choice as to what your heart calls out for you to do, and then you have the choice and the free will to create it and bring it into your experience. There is a difference of creating for the intention of experiencing creation and creating for the intention of experiencing a win. Either way you must own the experience of creation!

Think about when you began this pageant journey and you wanted so badly to experience the feeling of wearing a beautiful dress, dancing across the stage, and learning how to share your thoughts with the judges in the interview room. You were in control over the experience of that creation because all of those thoughts and feelings were under your control. Now that you have had the chance to experience all of those feelings, you want to know what it feels like to win a pageant and have the beautiful crown placed on your head. The experience of creation is much the same, because when you own the feeling of creating that very experience you want then the experience will follow.

If you own the feelings and thoughts of winning a pageant, then as you are practicing your walk and learning better communication skills, you still own the feeling of winning the pageant. Although you cannot control the outcome of the pageant, you can create the feeling of winning by allowing your thoughts to visualize yourself there on the center stage being crowned. You can experience the thrill of what it would feel like to hear your name called out as the winner and suddenly you notice that you are carrying yourself differently that you did before.

You will also notice that you feel more confident and your eye contact becomes more direct and your walk becomes more poised. By creating the thoughts and feelings of what it would feel like to win the pageant, you are in essence already creating the experience of it by owning it. Whether or not your judges actually crown you the winner that becomes irrelevant because you have already experienced what it would be like to win, and their opinion becomes less important.

You can do this with any experience you want to create in your life, by first applying your creative ability as a co-creator with God and owning your experience with or without another person's approval. The more you practice this technique, the better you will become at being a deliberate creator in your life. Your experiences will feel more genuine and you will ultimately feel more in control of your life, because you in fact are creating many of those experiences whether you are aware of it or not.

Own your truth first Sophia, and your actions will fall into place easily and align with all that you are meant to have in your life. Spend time listening to the sound of your own voice while it whispers through your soul, and notice what things make you feel love and what experiences and people bring fear into your life. The more you do this, the better your life journey will be. Allow yourself permission to dream bigger than you ever have before, because it is through our dreams that God allows us to soar to higher clouds. You owned your experience even before you won your pageant.

These same three letters connect with one another in their meaning in such a short word. It's the same three letters in the word that create your joy...O-w-N and W-O-N. The difference is in your perspective of what you want to see and how much you are willing to take ownership of those experiences in your life that are already "won," but have not yet experienced. Own your goals and treasure them like they are gold, because they represent limitless value to you. Own your dreams and step by step take accountability for bringing them into fruition until you finally see them manifest into your reality.

I have always loved you my beautiful daughter, even before you ever introduced yourself to me in my dreams. We are connected and no amount of time or distance will ever separate our love. Always remember Sophia that you and I are connected forever. I am so proud of you my precious child...and always remember that I am just a thought away.

I love you forever,

Momma

Sophia stared at the letter as her eyes filled with tears. All of these years of her mom's battle, all of these months of grief, and all of these past weeks of struggle finally began to make sense. Sophia remembered fondly the moments that she and her mom had before her mom passed away, and all her mom wanted was for Sophia to have the courage to turn this most painful experience into her greatest achievement. Sophia smiled as she stared at the roses that rested on her arms, and she felt like she had accomplished the greatest feat she had ever undertaken. Sophia battled depression and lack of faith in God which turned full circle and she was feeling joy beyond words and greater faith than she could ever imagine.

As Sophia heard the ringtones of her texts sharing with her congratulatory messages from friends and family, she closed her eyes and said a prayer in gratitude. *Thank you God. In my deepest time of sorrow you never left me, but it was I who left you. Thank you for your love and I now know that Momma is safe in your arms. Please give her a kiss for me and tell her that I miss her each and every day.* As Sophia's heart filled with joy, she inhaled and absorbed the overwhelming feelings that she was experiencing. The journey which she had taken from her mom's diagnosis to where she was at today felt more like a beginning of the journey instead of the end of it. She stared at the letter and then looked back up to the mirror filled with congratulatory messages written in lipstick, lip liner, and eye liner from her friends that she had shared the same dressing room with earlier that day.

Sophia smiled as she slowly folded the letter and placed it back into the envelope. As she heard a familiar ringtone, Sophia picked up her cell phone. "Hi Daddy," she said with a slight strain in her voice as she held back the tears. "We did it," she said and smiled. As Sophia listened to her dad congratulate her and promise her the largest pizza and ice cream celebration dinner, Sophia laughed. "Tell Miss Ariel thank you, and I will see you both as soon as I gather my things together." Slowly she placed the phone back on the makeup table and closed her eyes.

I love you momma this one is for you, Sophia thought and just as she opened her eyes she smelled the strong scent of roses. Sophia quickly looked at the roses lying on her lap and wondered why she had not noticed the strong aroma before now. Suddenly a chill filled the air and Sophia's skin turned ice cold, and as the aroma of roses grew stronger Sophia began to tremble. She looked up in the mirror in front of her to see the reflection of a beautiful woman smiling back at her. "Momma?" Sophia cried as she turned quickly to look behind her but nobody was there...she was all alone. Just then Sophia spun back around to see if she could find the reflection once again but it was gone.

As Sophia sat motionless in the chair, tears filled her eyes and the air grew even colder around her. Still staring into the mirror Sophia saw a smile begin to form on her tear stained face as she heard the most familiar voice she had ever known whisper into her ear, "I am so proud of you my precious child. Remember that I am always with you and I am just a thought away...I love you forever."

Now begins your journey...

Other Books by Suzy Bootz

Through the Eyes of Truth – A Conversation with God about My Life, Your Life, and Discovering Our Purpose – Available on Audible and on Amazon

Creating Utopia – Living Life as a Miracle Worker Available on Amazon

God Whispers – Daily Devotional for Inspired Living - Available on Amazon

Follow Us On:

Twitter: realsuzybootz

Instagram: realsuzybootz

To live inspired please visit www.suzybootz.com